Child of Joy

We Three Kings:

By

KIMBERLY RAE
JORDAN

THREE**STRAND**
P R E S S

A CORD OF THREE STRANDS IS NOT EASILY BROKEN.

A man, a woman & their God.
Three Strand Press publishes Christian Romance stories
that intertwine love, faith and family. Always clean.
Always heartwarming. Always uplifting.

Child of Joy/ Kimberly Rae Jordan. -- 1st ed.
ISBN-13: 978-1-988409-55-9

Now is your time of grief,
but I will see you again
and you will rejoice,
and no one will take away your joy.

John 16:22

CHAPTER 1

Carissa Jenkins tightened her hold on Rachel's hand as they stepped from the warmth of the babysitter's house into the frigid temperatures that held Minneapolis in its grip. It was far too early in the season to be experiencing such cold weather, which meant that winter, having started so early, would feel like it was dragging on forever.

As they walked, she glanced down to make sure that the scarf she'd fastened across the lower half of her daughter's face was still in place. Rachel hated having to wear a scarf and usually tugged it down. Thankfully, she hadn't touched it.

Carissa hurried them as fast as Rachel's short legs could carry her to their apartment that was a couple of blocks away. If only her car hadn't died after years of faithful service. She had no way to pay for the needed repairs, so it sat in her parking stall in the lot behind the apartment building. Just one more thing she was going to need to find a new place for.

The frigid air tightened the inside of her nose as she inhaled, and Carissa blinked against the cold that stung her eyes. If only she could have afforded to move them far, far away from the cold winters of Minnesota. Unfortunately, the chains of her pathetic finances held them firmly in place. She didn't even have enough money to move them to another apartment, which was exactly what she needed to do in just a few weeks.

"Hurry, Mama!" Rachel's words were muffled by the scarf, but the tug on her hand made Carissa realize she'd allowed herself to slow down as her thoughts had gotten bogged down in the mire of her situation.

They scurried along the sidewalk that had not been sufficiently cleared from the latest snowfall, Carissa trying her best to keep them both on their feet. Finally, their apartment building came into view, a gray block that blended in with the other gray blocks around it. Though she hated much about the rundown building, it had been their home for the past few years.

When they reached the outer security door, Carissa tugged it open and let Rachel in first before stepping in behind her. She let the door swing closed, effectively shutting out the wind but doing little to remove the chill from the air.

At one time—long before they'd moved in—a key had been needed to pass through the second door, and guests had been required to use the now-defunct intercom system to be buzzed into the building. Now, though, the door was permanently unlocked, allowing anyone who wanted to enter their gray apartment block to easily do so.

The building was eerily quiet as they made their way to the sagging steps—the elevator had never worked in all the time they'd lived there—and together, they avoided the places where there were dangerous gaps in the stairs. When they reached the fourth and top floor of the building, they moved across the threadbare carpet that was worn so thin it was non-existent in some spots.

Doors to the other apartments on the floor were closed, but Carissa knew that there was no one behind them. She was pretty sure the only other residents still in the building lived on the first and third floors. It was possible, however, that they, too, had moved out, and she had missed their departure. She was actually kind of surprised that no homeless people had taken up residence in the mostly abandoned building.

Soon, she and Rachel might be the only ones left in the building, with just five weeks left until they had to officially move out. Carissa still had no idea where they were going to go, but she did have a couple more leads to follow up on, and she prayed with all her heart that something would work out.

"Go sit on the couch, lovey," Carissa said, ushering Rachel toward the couch, still bundled up in her winterwear. Once her daughter was settled, she turned on the small space heater that she'd put on the one end table she had. "Sit there until it warms up a bit, okay?"

"Can I watch *Peppa Pig*, Mama?" Rachel nodded toward the old laptop that sat on the beat-up coffee table in front of her.

"Sure." It was one way to keep her from whining about being uncomfortable while they waited for the apartment to warm up.

It took Cassie a minute to set it up, then she went to the kitchen to make them some supper. The stove had stopped working a couple of months ago, but since they'd been given notice to move out, no repairs had been done. And certainly, no appliances were being replaced.

Thankfully, she'd found a single burner hot plate at the same thrift store where she'd gotten the space heater. It meant she could still cook meals for them. She opened the fridge to take out the small package of ground beef she'd pulled out of the freezer that morning to defrost. It was the last of a large, marked-down pack that she'd separated into smaller amounts and frozen a month ago.

She also took out the container of spaghetti sauce that she had frozen after using part of it a week or so ago. Though she would have liked to just dump the meat in the pan and add the sauce, Rachel loved meatballs.

Working quickly, Carissa added some salt and pepper to the meat then formed small balls, which she added to the pan that was heating on the stove. Her stomach rumbled as the smell of the cooking food filled the kitchen.

When the meatballs were cooked, she added the sauce and let it simmer for a bit as she filled a pot with water. Having only one burner made making multi-pot meals a bit of a challenge, so once the meatballs and sauce had simmered a bit, she moved the pan off the burner and put a lid on it. After putting the pot of water on the burner, she took a couple of dish towels from the drawer and wrapped them around the pot of sauce and meatballs.

"I'm warm now, Mama," Rachel called from across the room.

Carissa went over and helped her take off her winterwear, tucking her mitts, hat, and scarf into the coat sleeve of her jacket. She reached for the zip-up hoodie that was on the couch behind Rachel and helped her into it, zipping it up over the long-sleeve T-shirt she'd worn to school that day.

"Tuck your hands in the pockets," Carissa said, waiting until Rachel had done it before heading back to the kitchen to continue her supper preparations with the sounds of a little British pig playing in the background.

As she poured the last of a bag of peas into a bowl to heat in the small microwave, Carissa mentally reviewed the food she had left before she would need to go to the store again. Meal prep was one of the most stressful parts of her life currently. If it was just her, she would have lived off cheap ramen, and while there were days she did do just that, she never fed it to Rachel. Even that night, she would make sure Rachel ate her fill first, and if there wasn't enough left, she'd make some ramen for herself.

Once the noodles were cooked and strained, Carissa put some in a bowl and added meatballs and sauce. It would have been nice to have had some grated cheese or garlic toast to go with the spaghetti. But Rachel had never had those things as part of the meal, so she wouldn't miss them.

She carried the bowl over to the coffee table and set it down, then returned to get Rachel a small glass of milk and a TV tray. Once she was all set up, Carissa paused the show on the laptop. Rachel made a sound of protest even though she knew the drill.

Rachel said a prayer of thanks then dug into the bowl of food. As she ate, Carissa asked about her day at school, then listened with a smile as in between bites, Rachel happily shared what she'd done.

After she'd finished the one bowl, she asked for a bit more. Carissa was just heading back to the kitchen when there was a knock on her door. Her heart began to pound since it was so rare that anyone came by. Fear for her daughter had Carissa setting the bowl down and motioning for Rachel to follow her to the bathroom.

"Stay here and be quiet until I say you can come out, okay?" Carissa whispered, then locked the handle and pulled it closed behind her as she heard another knock.

Back at the door, she made sure the chain lock was on, then opened it.

Hunter King got out of the car and pulled up the collar of his coat, trying to block the wind that whipped down the street. When he spotted a man standing in the doorway of the apartment building, he headed his way, eager to be out of the frigid cold. It wasn't supposed to get this cold before January, but apparently, nature hadn't gotten the message because here they were, the last week of November, freezing every time they stepped outside.

"Hey there," Stan Edgemire said as Hunter approached.

"Thanks so much for meeting me on such short notice." Hunter shook the man's hand. "My mom wants me to weigh in on decisions regarding things that I have no clue about. I needed a reason to be out of the building and tied up for a little while."

Stan chuckled as they moved into the apartment block. "What's she getting after you for?"

"That would be the women and children's shelter fundraiser tomorrow night," Hunter said. "Why she thinks I'm the logical person to go to for the last-minute details of the event, I have no idea. She'd be much better off going to Heather."

"She's likely going to both of you."

Stan was probably right. But still, Hunter had needed to escape the office. She could still reach him by phone, but he'd left his cell in the car for the time being. "You're attending the fundraiser, right?"

The older man nodded with a smile. "My wife is really looking forward to it. I think it's the highlight of the year. Mainly because she knows she can go buy herself a new dress and shoes, and I'm not gonna say anything about it."

Hunter looked around as they moved further inside the building, frowning as he took in the dreary and darkened interior. He was glad that they were coming close to the date for demolition of the building.

"How many residents are left?" He wanted the answer to be none, but he knew that wasn't the case.

"Four, but one is moving out next week."

"And the other three?"

Stan gave a shrug. "I've tried to get answers from them, but they appear to be holding out until the bitter end."

Hunter felt a frisson of annoyance. They had given the residents ten months' notice to be out by the end of the year, plus two months rent-free so that they could save up for relocation expenses. There should have been no one left in the block at this point. That there were still people living there concerned him because they had been doing the absolute minimum when it came to repairs on the building. There was no sense in dumping money into a building that was going to be demolished.

They had let the residents know that when they'd served them notice nine months earlier. There had been a fairly quick exodus by quite a few of the residents, but somehow, they needed to encourage the remaining ones to move sooner rather than later.

"The guy on this floor is an older gentleman," Stan said as they walked along the worn carpet of the dark hallway. "He's lived here for more than ten years."

Stan knocked on the door, then stepped back, waiting for an answer. It didn't take long for the door to open a crack, revealing a portion of a scowling face.

Five minutes later, Hunter was aggravated. The older man had been grouchy and unwilling to divulge his plans. He hadn't even acknowledged that he had to be out of the building by the end of December. Hunter had a feeling that that tenant was going to be a challenge.

Thankfully, the second visit went much better. That renter said he had plans to be out by the fifteenth. He actually thanked Hunter for all the notice plus the two months of free rent. It helped to soothe some of the aggravation, but he was still on edge.

Maybe he should have stuck to fielding his mother's calls about the fundraiser.

"I'm a bit concerned about this final one," Stan said, a frown creasing his brow. "She's a single mom with a young daughter. I really don't think she's managed to find a place. From what I understood the few times I've spoken with her, she's had a run of bad luck. Her car quit, then she lost one of her jobs."

Hunter followed the man to the fourth floor then down the hallway to a plain door. Stan knocked, but though Hunter heard noise behind the door, it didn't open, so Stan knocked again.

Finally, the door cracked open, a chain stretching across the opening as a woman's slender face appeared.

"Hello, Ms. Jenkins," Stan said, his voice warm and friendly. "How are you doing?"

"I'm fine. How are you?"

The woman's voice was soft and low. Her gaze met Hunter's for a moment, and he saw that her eyes were an odd mix of blue and green and framed by long, dark lashes. Her skin was quite fair, and there were dark smudges beneath her eyes.

"I'm good. This is Hunter King, the owner of the building." Her gaze darted to Hunter again, her eyes growing wider. "He's come by to make sure there are no issues with your move-out. Have you found another place for you and your daughter yet?"

Her fingers crept around the edge of the door, her knuckles going white as she gripped it. "Not yet, but I have a couple leads I'll be following up on soon."

"Do you at least have an option if those leads don't pan out by the end December?" Hunter asked.

Her hesitation told him everything he needed to know, and the worry in her gaze did weird things to his stomach.

"I'll figure something out."

"I'm sure you will," Stan said, his tone soothing. It was clear this woman triggered a protective response from the older man. "We'll be back by to check on you again. Is there anything you need? Any issues you're having with the apartment?"

Another hesitation before she shook her head. "We're fine."

"You take care then, okay?" Stan appeared to wait for her nod before he said goodbye.

As they walked toward the stairs, Hunter glanced back at the closed door. There appeared to be no heat in the hallway. Given

e only reason he could think of why people would still be
was that they had nowhere else to go. If that was the case,
e just couldn't turn his back on them.

ally putting his car in gear, Hunter pulled away from the
knowing that if his mother wasn't so caught up in the plans
: fundraiser, he'd be seeking her out instead of trying to
ner. But come Sunday afternoon, he'd be paying a visit to
ome she shared with his sister, Heather, who was the
st of the three King siblings, though only by a few minutes.

ne residents in the building had no options, he needed to
up with some for them if possible. Though he hadn't been
: who had owned the building during the time when it had
rated, he was the one who owned it now. The cost to bring
• habitable conditions would have been almost as much as
g a new one from scratch, which was why it was being
shed and a new one would be built in its place.

d understood that even in its deplorable condition, the
; was home to people. Still, it wasn't until a few minutes
: those people had names and faces. Now he had a hard
tting the wizened face of the older man and the wide,
blue-green gaze of the woman out of his head.

ter had a feeling that until he did something about their
n, he wouldn't be able to forget them.

the state of the building in general, he w
apartment wasn't much better off. Was i
the woman and her child?

When he'd had Stan notify the reside
pending demolition shortly after he'd p
thought that nine months later, they'd
residence. He'd hoped that the long n
wouldn't have any issues to deal with w
rolled around.

Apparently, he'd been dead wrong on

"What are the chances they'll all be
first?"

"Well, at least two will be out before
Stan shrugged. "I'm not sure what to sa
any shape to house people. But I think
have nowhere else to go, it's better that
out of the elements."

"You said there's a child in the apart

Stan nodded. "I'm not a great judg
think she's probably five or six years ol

Hunter was still mulling over what
tenants weren't out by the end of De
the front door. He shook Stan's hand
for meeting me here for this check-up.

"You're welcome. I'll come by ag
with the ones without plans in place."

"Let me know what you find out."

"Will do." With a nod of his head
Hunter walked to his SUV and
turned the vehicle on but didn't put i
at the building, cataloging all the wa
people to be living, especially the you

T
there
then
Fi
curb,
for th
avoid
the h
youn
If
come
the on
deteri
it up t
buildi
demo
He
buildi
ago th
time p
fearful
Hu
situatio

CHAPTER 2

Carissa's legs were trembling as she made her way from the door to the bathroom. The adrenaline that had rushed through her at the sound of the knock was slowly ebbing away, leaving in its wake a shakiness she didn't appreciate. Her greatest fear was that despite all her best efforts to provide a loving and caring home for her daughter, someone would judge those efforts as not good enough and take Rachel from her.

She wasn't sure she'd survive if that happened. As it stood, everything she did, she did for Rachel. Every job she'd ever taken had been to provide food and a home for her daughter. Carissa couldn't allow herself to consider that, in the end, it wasn't enough.

Carissa rested her head against the bathroom door and took a deep breath, holding it for a moment before she exhaled. "Knock. Knock."

Hesitation then, "Who's there?"

"Mama Bear." As the handle slowly turned, she straightened and looked down into her daughter's heart-shaped face. "You can come out now."

"Who was it?" Rachel asked as she reached for Carissa's hand. Fear lingered in her eyes—so close in color to her own.

"It was just someone from the company that owns the building."

"Did you tell them it's cold in here? That sometimes I can see my breath?"

"I think they know." Carissa led her back to the couch and the warmth of the heater. "But we're going to be moving soon, so it won't be a problem anymore."

At least she hoped that was the case. Presumably, if they ended up in a shelter somewhere, it would be warm, even if they had to share a room with strangers.

"Can we decorate the tree tonight?" Excitement at the prospect pushed back the last of the fear that had been lingering on her tiny features.

"I think we can." Carissa reached out and let her fingers drift down Rachel's soft cheek, pushing back strands of blonde hair that had escaped her braids. "How about you eat the rest of your supper, then we'll set up the tree before bed."

"Okay!"

Carissa returned to the kitchen and added more food to Rachel's bowl. There was enough left for a bowl for herself, and since she was sure that Rachel would be full Carissa went ahead and dished up some for herself.

Rachel continued to alternate between bites of food and sharing tidbits of her day at school. Carissa was glad that school wasn't a battle with Rachel. The girl loved her teacher and loved to learn. Her intelligence had allowed her to skip a grade already, and Carissa hoped that one day, Rachel's smarts would keep her from ending up in circumstances like they were currently enduring.

Once their food was gone, Carissa let Rachel watch one more episode of *Peppa Pig* while she cleaned up the kitchen, then went to get the beat-up plastic tub where she stored all their Christmas things.

There wasn't much, but each year, once the tree was up, Carissa allowed Rachel to choose a decoration at the thrift store to add to what they had. Though money was tighter than ever, she would find a way to continue the tradition.

She knew that Rachel would have memories of cold winter days and sweltering summer nights, of not always being able to have the treats she wanted. But Carissa hoped that amongst the not-so-great memories would linger thoughts of the small traditions they'd shared together.

Their tree was small, and fewer lights on the single strand she had worked than the year before. Still, Rachel didn't seem to notice as she carefully hung their assortment of decorations on the spindly branches. When that was done, Carissa helped her arrange the small skirt over the plastic tree stand.

"It looks so beautiful, Mama," Rachel said after Carissa turned off the light for the living room. The tree glowed softly in the semi-darkness, and Carissa decided it would be enough. It had to be enough.

Carissa was exhausted as she and Rachel made their way home one day later that week. The wind wasn't blowing as strongly, and the temperature had risen enough that the cold wasn't as bitter. Still, it took effort to walk along the sidewalk, trudging through the snow that had fallen steadily throughout the day. It seemed that so far that winter, it was either freezing cold or snowing. She just wanted a break from it all, and the winter wasn't even half over.

That day, she'd ended up with a double shift at the diner where she worked. Instead of just the breakfast/lunch shift, she'd worked through dinner as well. Given her current financial predicament, she was glad for the extra money. Thankfully, the babysitter had been willing to keep Rachel until she was done the second shift. Of course, Carissa had had to pay her extra, but in the end, she still came out ahead for having worked the shift.

Tips from the dinner crowd were usually higher, but her desire to be home in the evening with Rachel prevented her from taking that shift regularly. She was grateful for the job, even if it wasn't in the best restaurant around nor the best part of the city. The owners were understanding about her being a single mom and rarely messed with her shifts or gave her hassles on those rare days she'd needed time off if Rachel was sick.

The babysitter she left Rachel with had a couple of kids who went to the same school as Rachel, so she was willing to watch her before and after school. She also kept her rates reasonable, usually only charging extra when she was required to provide a meal.

It was just another reason why Carissa hated the thought of moving. Since she'd tried most of the apartment blocks within the area to no avail, a move was likely going to mean a change of babysitter and a change of school for Rachel. Her heart ached at the thought, knowing Rachel would be devastated to leave her favorite teacher and her friends.

Feeling anger begin to lick at the edges of her mind, Carissa tried to push the thought aside as she hurried Rachel along the sidewalk then up the stairs to the front door of the building. They had just stepped into the dreary foyer near the stairs when she heard her name being called.

~*~

"Ms. Jenkins?"

Hunter waited for the woman to turn, careful not to crowd too close to her. The last thing he wanted was for her to feel threatened by him. He just hoped that Heather's presence would help to ease any alarm the woman might feel.

"Yes?" She turned to face him, and once again, Hunter was struck by her eyes. Not just the color but the distinct wariness in her gaze.

"I'm Hunter King. We met the other day." He held out his hand, and after a moment of hesitation, she took it, her smaller hand getting lost in his large grip. After giving it a gentle shake, Hunter didn't prolong the contact. "This is my sister, Heather."

The woman's gaze moved from him to Heather, and she took his sister's hand when she offered it.

"It's nice to meet you," Heather said, her tone gentle. He'd warned her that Carissa Jenkins appeared to be a bit skittish, so he was glad that his sister was approaching her with caution as well.

Hunter looked down at the girl standing at Carissa's side. She was bundled up to her eyes in winter wear, but like her mom, she had incredible eyes that were huge in her tiny face. He thought about asking the girl's name, but he'd rather Carissa offer that information herself.

They were there that day, not to scare her but to make a connection that might allow them to help Carissa and her daughter. He also hoped to talk to the older gentleman who had been belligerent and stubborn about revealing his plans to move.

"We were wondering if there was anything you need in the apartment to help make it more comfortable until you move out," Heather asked. "We realize that things haven't been repaired as they might have been otherwise, given the pending demolition date."

"It's cold."

Hunter looked back at the young girl. She met his gaze head-on even as her mom admonished her softly. "Rachel."

Her gaze shifted to her mom. "But she asked, Mama. It's not nice when it's cold." Rachel looked back at Hunter. "I have to wear my jacket and boots when I get home from school until the heater makes it warm enough. I sit really close to it to stay warm. And we have to sleep with sweaters and lotsa blankets."

Hunter looked at Carissa, his heart clenching at the sadness he saw on her face as she regarded her daughter. He glanced at Heather, their gazes meeting and holding for a moment before they turned their attention back to the two people in front of them.

"Is there anything else?" Hunter asked, keeping his attention on Rachel. He figured that she might be more forthcoming than her mother would be about their current situation.

Rachel nodded. "The stove stopped working, so Mama can only cook on a small one."

Carissa's shoulders slumped like it was her failing that had caused these issues when Hunter knew that wasn't the case.

"Do you have hot water?" Heather asked. "For showers and washing dishes?"

Rachel was the one to answer again. "Mama makes the water hot on the stove then puts it in the bathtub for me."

"Okay," Hunter said, resisting the urge to take a deep breath to ease the band that had tightened around his chest. "We'll see what we can do to help with those things."

"Really?" Carissa asked, her gaze wide as she looked at him. "But we're supposed to be moving out."

"Yes, but until you do, it's our responsibility to make sure your living conditions are safe, especially for your daughter."

Hunter suspected that the way to get Carissa to agree to anything would be to play the *daughter* card. Just from their few minutes of conversation, he got the feeling that everything Carissa did was for her daughter, and the fact that they hadn't moved out told him that their situation was quite dire. He felt fairly confident that if she had the ability to move her daughter out of an apartment with little heat and no hot water, she would have done so already.

"When is the best time to reach you?" Heather asked.

Carissa shifted her attention to his sister. "I usually get home around four o'clock, and then we're home for the evening. We're also here on the weekend."

"Could I get your phone number?" Heather pulled her cell out of her pocket. "So that we can contact you just to confirm when someone will be by to deal with the issues in the apartment?"

With a nod, Carissa recited a number. Heather entered it into her phone, then a moment later, there was a ping sound from Carissa's pocket.

"There." Heather looked up from her phone and smiled at Carissa. "Now you have my number as well. If anything else comes up, please contact me. Okay?"

Though Carissa nodded, Hunter suspected she wouldn't.

"We won't keep you," Hunter said. "Thank you for your time."

Rachel lifted a mittened hand and tugged her scarf down, tucking it beneath her chin. She gave him a beaming smile and a tiny wave. "Bye."

The two of them headed for the stairs, and Hunter watched as Carissa led Rachel up the stairs, carefully guiding her past certain spots before the two of them disappeared on the second floor.

"This is absolutely disgraceful," Heather stated as they stood there, and Hunter couldn't disagree with her.

"Brace yourself," he said. "We still have one more resident to visit."

Carissa hadn't been sure what to think after the unexpected meeting with Hunter and Heather King. She'd only had a fleeting glimpse of Hunter through the crack in the door when he'd visited her apartment with the property manager. Seeing him standing there, his dark hair perfectly styled, dressed in a long black wool coat with an elegant scarf around his neck, she'd been struck by how out of place he looked. The only person who had looked *more* out of place had been his sister in her aubergine-colored coat and high-heeled black boots.

Carissa hadn't been pleased with Rachel so readily spilling all the details of their living situation with the pair, but she hadn't stopped her. If there had been any chance it might improve things for Rachel, she had to accept the embarrassment that came with the revelation that she couldn't provide better for her daughter.

Even though she allowed herself a tiny bit of hope that things might change for the better, Carissa wasn't holding her breath. That probably explained why she was surprised when she heard Heather's voice on the other end of the line when she answered her phone on Monday evening.

"Hi, Ms. Jenkins. This is Heather King."

"Hi. How are you?" she asked.

"I'm well. Thank you. And how are you and Rachel doing?"

"We're fine." That was stretching it a bit, but they were no worse off than they'd been recently. Nothing more had broken down in the apartment, and the temperatures hadn't plunged to frigid levels again. "Oh, and please call me Carissa."

"Okay, and you must call me Heather," she said, her voice friendly and warm. "I'm calling to see if you'd be available for a couple of people to come by tomorrow evening to check over the situation in the apartment."

"That's fine. We should be home all evening."

"Perfect. We'll be there then. If you think of anything more that needs attention, please make a note of it and let us know while we're there."

"Okay."

They said goodbye, then Carissa lowered the phone to her lap, thinking over what else she might be able to tell Heather, but nothing came to mind. For Carissa, the things Rachel had brought up were the most pressing. If the apartment was warmer and they had hot water again, she could deal with everything else.

Grocery shopping was looming, so she'd been pouring over the flyers from the nearby stores hoping to find the best deals on the food they needed. It was hard to avoid the sections of the flyers that advertised all the Christmas goodies and the toys. She'd managed to pick up a couple of small things that she hoped Rachel would like.

But despite her best efforts, there wouldn't be much under the tree or in her stocking this year. Thankfully, the tree was small, and so was the stocking, so the lack wasn't as evident as it might have been with a huge tree and a larger stocking.

Maybe one day, she'd have more to offer her daughter, but some days it felt like her prayers were going unanswered in that regard. And while God hadn't yet provided them with a place that they could afford, she believed that He had sent Heather and Hunter King their way to help make the apartment more habitable for the time they would still be there. For that, she was extremely grateful to Him.

The next afternoon, Carissa and Rachel hustled home from the babysitter. She knew that Rachel would be hungry, so she quickly made her a grilled cheese sandwich, promising that if she was still hungry, she could have some soup after the people left. With that and her own meal in mind, Carissa took a container out of the freezer.

She'd lucked onto a bunch of clearance vegetables a few weeks back and had brought them home and made a large batch of vegetable soup. Then, as she did with most things, she'd frozen it in smaller containers. It was almost gone now, and Carissa prayed she might find more vegetables so that she could make another batch. Soup was the perfect meal when it was so cold.

A little after five, Carissa heard a knock on the door. She quickly set a glass of milk on the TV tray in front of Rachel. "Say a prayer for your food, okay, sweetie? I need to answer the door."

Since she was expecting this visit, Carissa didn't send Rachel to the bathroom in a panic. She left the chain in place until she confirmed who was at the door, then she released the chain and opened the door fully to allow the strangers into her home.

CHAPTER 3

Hunter wasn't sure why he'd insisted on coming along, but Heather was there too, so perhaps he didn't need to give an explanation. They could have just arranged for Stan to show up with the people who needed to take care of things in the apartment. The items they'd brought with them remained in the hallway for the time being.

There was hardly a difference in temperature from the hallway as they stepped into the apartment. He noticed that Carissa still wore her coat, and when he spotted Rachel, he saw she did as well. When Rachel's gaze met his, she gave a little wave before turning her attention back to the food in front of her.

"Hello, Carissa," Heather said, holding out her hand.

Carissa shook it quickly then clasped her hands together as she regarded them with wary eyes. "I don't know what you need to see, but feel free to look around."

As they stepped further into the apartment, Hunter's gaze swept around the open space. It was small, but that was probably better if they were trying to keep it warm with a space heater.

He spotted a tiny Christmas tree with lights on the end table next to Rachel. There were no presents under it, but a small stocking hung off the edge of the table the tree sat on.

When he thought of the huge trees—yes, trees plural—they had at his family home, along with the tree his mom insisted he have at the apartment he shared with Hayden, a pit opened in the bottom of his stomach. His family had always been charitable, supporting worthy causes around the city that included shelters and food banks, as well as having fundraisers for those places like they'd had not long ago. This was, however, the first time someone's need had been so in his face.

He wanted to ask so many questions. Where was Rachel's father? Did Carissa not have family who could help her out? What had happened that had led her to this situation?

But even though the questions sat on the tip of his tongue, he held them back. It wasn't any of his business, really. What *was* his business was the condition of the building, so that was what he tried to focus on right then.

They'd already determined that it would be easier to use space heaters for the next few weeks, rather than try to replace the heating unit for the building. They'd brought three for Carissa's apartment, and three for the other gentleman who had yet to reveal his plans to leave.

They'd also decided to get in-shower hot water heaters. That seemed to be the best solution for the short time they were needed. And finally, there was a new stove for both apartments. They hadn't purchased super high-end stoves, but they were still good quality. When they were no longer needed, they'd donate them to someplace that provided furniture to people in need.

The man installing the hot water heater would have to come back another day, however. But hopefully, Carissa would be okay with having people in her apartment while she wasn't there in order for them to complete the work. That night, they'd brought people to help set up the space heaters and get the stove in place and functional.

"Do you mind if we have a bit of a look around to see how to best set up the heaters?" Heather asked.

As the oldest child, Hunter usually took the lead on most things, and he'd been the one to speak to the other tenant. However, when it came to Carissa, for some reason, he felt she'd be more receptive to interacting with Heather. He knew he could come across as imposing, and the last thing he wanted to do was make her feel uncomfortable.

"Sure," Carissa said with a nod, wrapping her arms across her waist.

He couldn't wait for them to get the heaters up and running so that Carissa and Rachel could take their coats off. Rachel looked like a little pufflelump in all her winter gear while she nibbled on a sandwich, her eyes wide as she watched them.

Hunter followed the man who would set up the heaters down the hallway to the bedroom. There was a double bed against one wall and a beat-up dresser against the opposite one. There were two pillows on the mattress and a couple of blankets lay across it as well. The pit in his stomach grew as he imagined the two of them huddling under the blankets trying to keep warm.

"I think we should put it in the corner here." The man gestured to a spot on the far side of the room near the window. "That would be the best place to cut the cold and circulate warm air in the room."

Hunter had no knowledge to argue that logic, so he just nodded. "Will this push enough warm air to the hallway and the bathroom?"

"If we get enough heat circulating with the three heaters, it should be. But if not, we can put a smaller one in the hallway directing it toward the bathroom."

He wanted the apartment to be so filled with warmth that they never had to wear their coats inside again. So whatever that would take, he was willing to do.

~*~

Carissa went and sat beside Rachel on the couch while Hunter and Heather King gave directions to the people they'd brought with them. After a quick tour of the apartment, they began carting in boxes, and then they used a two-wheeler to bring in what appeared to be a new stove.

Were they really going to replace the broken stove with a brand new one? She could hardly believe that, and from the look of things, they had brought several heaters to put around the apartment. The idea of finally being warm in their home almost made her giddy. Last winter, they'd still had a bit of heat in the apartment. But this year, when the weather had turned cold, it was apparent that whatever last leg the heating system had been standing on, had given out.

Knowing what was to come of the building, and the fact that it was already almost empty, Carissa had assumed that they wouldn't do anything to repair it. And while that assumption appeared to be correct, it seemed that they were willing to do other things to help alleviate the issue.

"How is the fridge working?" Heather asked from the kitchen.

Carissa got to her feet and went to join the woman. "Seems okay. It keeps stuff frozen in the freezer and cold in the fridge as far as I can tell."

"Well, that could be because the apartment has been so cold. That might be masking whether there is a real issue or not. You may notice a difference once it's warmer in here." Heather opened the fridge and bent, appearing to check the settings.

Carissa tried not to be embarrassed that the only things in the fridge were a nearly empty jug of milk, a container of eggs that was down to the last two, and a jar of jam. The freezer wasn't much better. There was a loaf of day-old bread that she'd picked up on sale and frozen so it would last longer and one last container of soup.

"If you notice a change once the apartment is warmer, give me a call." Heather looked over at her, a determined gaze on her face. "Okay?"

Carissa nodded. "I'll let you know."

"Good. Now, let's move so this guy can get the stove set up."

It had been unboxed, and the man was piling the packing material all together, clearly waiting for them to get out of the way.

As they left him to his work, Heather headed over to sit next to Rachel. Smiling down at her, she said, "Are you excited for Christmas?"

Rachel nodded as she picked up her glass. "I wrote a letter to Santa."

Carissa looked at her in surprise. "You did?"

"When you were getting the water ready for my bath last night."

"Would you like me to mail it to Santa for you?" Heather asked.

"You don't have to do that," Carissa said.

Heather shrugged. "It's not a problem. Saves you having to find a mailbox. We have mail collection right at the office."

"You'll make sure Santa gets it?" Rachel asked, an eager look on her face.

"Of course." Heather gave her a warm smile. "I know how important it is to Santa to get all the letters that are sent to him."

Rachel clasped her hands under her chin, her delight clear. "Thank you so much!"

"You're welcome."

"I'm done, Mama," Rachel said. "Can I get up now?"

"Yes." Carissa had a feeling that Rachel was going to get whatever was on that list if she was entrusting it to Heather King. Perhaps they were about to become the Kings' charity project.

A part of Carissa rebelled against the idea. She didn't want to have to rely on other people to provide things like Christmas presents for her daughter. But sadly, the reality was that that year, she needed the help more than ever.

The past four years had been a steady decline in what she'd been able to do for Rachel at Christmas. At the same time, Rachel's awareness of what her friends got versus what she got had increased. Maybe this year, with a bit of help if she could put her pride away, it might be a Christmas Rachel would remember fondly in years to come.

Rachel knelt down by the end table and pulled out the small box that contained her crayons and the books and papers she used to color and draw. She opened it and drew out a folded piece of paper. Carissa wished she could see what was written on it, but Rachel took it right to Heather and held it out.

"I don't have an envelope," she said.

Heather took the paper with a warm smile. "No worries. I can take care of that for you."

"Thank you." Rachel beamed up at her. "I can't wait for Christmas morning!"

Carissa bit her lip at her words. What if they didn't plan to follow through with the list? Maybe Heather would just put it in an envelope and put it in the mail. Carissa would have to try to figure out what Rachel had included, so she could at least get one thing off of it, if at all possible.

Her stomach clenched at the idea of what Christmas morning would be like if she couldn't figure out what Rachel wanted.

"Is there anything else that you need help with?" This question came from Hunter when the last of the space heaters had been set up.

Carissa tried not to squirm under his intense scrutiny. His blue eyes reminded her of pictures she'd seen of the clear waters of the Pacific. Framed by dark lashes and heavy eyebrows, his gaze was direct and piercing.

This time, however, her pride did kick in. Now that she had heat, hot water, and a way to cook food for Rachel, she could manage the rest.

"No. We're fine."

His brow lifted slightly at her words, and she knew he likely didn't consider their situation *fine*, but it was the best it could be given their current circumstances. Circumstances that he wouldn't be able to change for them.

"If anything else comes up, please let Heather or I know."

Like she had with Heather, Carissa gave a single nod. These two people had been more generous than they'd needed to be, and she was grateful for that. She wouldn't be greedy since what they had now was one hundred percent better than what they'd had.

Hunter pulled his gloves from the pocket of his coat and headed for the door. He'd taken a couple steps in that direction when he turned back around.

"By the way," he began. "There will be no rent payment due for December."

"Really?" Carissa felt a band that had been slowly tightening around her chest as the first of the month loomed, loosen.

Hunter nodded. "Really. We are extending an additional month to you and the other remaining tenants. Hopefully, that will help you find a place."

Carissa's throat tightened, and her eyes stung with tears. She looked away and blinked rapidly. "Thank you."

Hunter cleared his throat. "You're welcome, and again, let us know if there's something else you need. Stan Edgemire will be by tomorrow during the day with the man to install the hot water heater in your shower. Hopefully that will be okay."

"That's fine," Carissa assured him. She trusted the older man as she'd been dealing with him for the last several months, and he'd always been kind to her and Rachel.

The brother-sister pair then said goodnight, and within minutes, everyone had left, and it was just her and Rachel.

"Can I take my jacket off now?" Rachel asked.

The air in the apartment had definitely warmed, so she nodded. "Are you still hungry?"

"Nope." Rachel said. "I'm full."

"Okay. Are you ready to read?"

Now that Rachel was in grade three, there was more reading, but thankfully, she loved books. As did Carissa, so while Rachel had school reading to do each night, they were also working their way through a series of books that Rachel had picked out from the library.

In the warmth of their apartment, they curled up side-by-side on the couch and together escaped into someone else's world. Carissa knew that the rough times weren't over, but at that moment, she felt a sense of peace and contentment.

For the first time in what felt like forever, hope flickered within her heart. Since an accident had irrevocably changed their lives, hope had been hard to find. Becoming a single mom not long out of high school had been a big enough struggle. But completely losing her support system four years earlier had devastated her and left her floundering.

And she'd never quite gotten past that floundering. Every day it felt like she was just desperately trying to keep from drowning. Finally, though, she felt like she could breathe without the threat of getting a mouthful of water.

Even if it was just for the day.

CHAPTER 4

"Read this." Heather held out a folded piece of paper, then turned to look out the window as their driver pulled away from the curb.

Hunter didn't often utilize George, the family driver. However, since he'd still needed to make calls and touch base with people while out of the office, he'd had the man meet them to drive them to the dilapidated building.

"What is it?" he asked as he unfolded the paper.

Heather didn't respond, just continued to stare out the window. Hunter frowned as he read the words written in green and red pencil crayon that absolutely filled the page in small, neatly printed letters.

Dear Santa,

I have tried my best to be super good this year because I wanted to be able to ask you for some things.

I would really like new boots. The ones I have now pinch my toes but I don't want to tell Mama because she'll be sad.

I would also love some chapter books. Reading is my favorite thing and we can't always go to the library.

My mom has been good this year too so I want to ask for something for her too. I think she really needs a good husband. My friend Mandi says her dad does stuff for her mom, and it makes her mom happy. I want my mom to be happy like that too. I try to do stuff to make her happy but I'm only eight and have no money.

Maybe you know someone who's been good and needs a wife. My mom is the best mom ever so I know she'll be a good wife too.

And if you can't find her a husband, maybe you could get her a laptop. Hers is old and keeps shutting down when we want to watch videos on YouTube or when she tries to do stuff on it.

Thank you for reading my letter. I hope you have a GREAT day!

Love ~ Rachel Joy Jenkins

P.S. My mom's name is Carissa Jenkins.

Hunter swallowed against the emotions rising up inside him as he handed the paper back to Heather. He wasn't sure why this young girl was getting to him. In recent years, December had become a difficult month for him. For their whole family, actually. This would be their fourth Christmas without their dad, and it was still horribly hard.

Christmas had been his dad's favorite time of the year, and he had been looking forward to having grandchildren to celebrate with now that his own kids were adults. It was why he'd always had a huge children's Christmas party for the employees in their companies. He'd dress up as Santa and have fun handing out gifts to the employees' kids.

Each employee was encouraged to submit a gift idea for their child or children in the twenty-five-dollar range. His mom and sister along with a couple of assistants would happily do the shopping, then his dad would give the gifts out at the party. Though they'd continued the tradition of the Christmas party even in his father's absence, Hunter hadn't been able to bring himself to fill the role of Santa.

His dad would have loved Rachel, and he would have likely granted every wish on her list and then some, considering she'd only asked for two things for herself.

"We'll have to get those things for her," Hunter said, his throat tight. Well, except for the husband. Not much they could do about that. However, they could get her mom a laptop.

"And a few extra things too," Heather added.

He let out a sigh as he shifted in his seat. The pain of missing his father, of trying to step into his shoes in so many ways, bloomed from the dull ache that usually sat in his chest to a pain that couldn't be ignored. He rubbed at his chest, wishing he could alleviate the pain.

"At least they'll be warm tonight, and they can cook on a full stove instead of a single burner hot plate," Heather said.

"I feel like I failed Dad by not being more aware of the tenants' situations. If he saw the way Rachel was living, he would have been horrified."

"But he also would have admired Carissa for doing everything she could to protect her daughter."

That would have been true. Their dad had been raised in poverty by a single mom, so he would have seen himself in that situation. He'd worked hard to build the business empire that had passed on to Hunter and his siblings upon his death.

"Maybe we should invite her and Carissa to the children's party," Heather suggested after a few minutes of silence. "I bet she'd really like that."

"If you think we should, I'll leave the invite up to you."

"I think I will extend the invitation," Heather said. "I'll have to figure out what to get for her beyond the books and boots she asked for."

"The boots are a bit too practical for the party, but the books might be okay."

"Part of me wants to get her something like an iPad, but that wouldn't be fair to the other kids."

Hunter looked over at Heather. "If you want to get her that, I'm not going to say no. But yeah, I don't think it would be appropriate to give it to her at the children's party."

"I'll call Carissa later and make arrangements for the party. She might need a ride, so if she does, we'll send George to pick her up."

Hunter nodded. Heather had a few days to convince Carissa to come to the party. The one thing that might help her accept the invite was the fact that it was a party for Rachel, and it appeared that Carissa would do most anything for her daughter.

~*~

Carissa had figured she'd seen the last of Heather and Hunter King once everything was dealt with at the apartment. There had been no reason for Heather to contact Carissa again, and Carissa had had no intention of bothering her or Hunter again. So the phone call, when it came later that evening, was a bit of a surprise.

"I want to extend an invitation to you and Rachel to attend the children's Christmas party that our company is hosting."

"A Christmas party?"

"Yep. We host it each year, and we'd love to have Rachel there this year."

Carissa wanted to say yes because Rachel would love to attend a Christmas party. But that would mean a nice outfit, and Rachel didn't have one since she hadn't really needed something like that. Unfortunately, Carissa didn't have the money to buy one either.

"Why don't you think about it?" Heather said when Carissa didn't respond right away. "Then let me know. You don't have to worry about getting there. We'll make sure you have a ride there and back home again."

Oh, the temptation was definitely strong. She knew without a doubt that Rachel would be over the moon to attend a Christmas party.

"I'll let you know."

"Wonderful! I hope you can both make it. It's a children's party, but the parents come with the kids."

Great...so that meant she'd need an outfit for herself too.

After Heather hung up, Carissa went to check on Rachel. She was in bed reading, but it was almost time for her to go to sleep. It was so nice to not be worried about how cold the bedroom was anymore, because it wasn't. The whole apartment was blissfully warm.

"Time for sleep, lovey," Carissa said as she sat down on the edge of the bed.

She held out her hand, and Rachel took it. Together, they said her nighttime prayer, taking turns to pray for certain things. When they were done, Carissa pressed a kiss to her forehead then sat back, staring down at her.

"Are you sure you don't want to tell me what was in your letter to Santa?"

"I'm positive, Mama. It's just for him to read."

Carissa decided not to point out that Heather had likely read her letter, and possibly Hunter had as well. "If you change your mind, I'd love to hear what you wrote."

Rachel shook her head, her hair sliding against her pillow. "Nope."

She couldn't help but smile at the stubborn determination on Rachel's little face. "Okay. Sleep well."

Leaving Rachel alone to sleep, Carissa went back to the kitchen to clean up and prepare for the next day. She needed to make a grocery list. At one time, she shopped according to a menu she created for the week. Now she had to make a menu from whatever she found on sale and the few necessities she didn't like to be without.

She sat on the couch, reveling in the warmth that permeated the room. Previously, in the evenings, she'd had to either go into the bedroom with Rachel, where she'd moved the heater, or put on a thick sweater to try to ward off the cold in the other rooms of the apartment.

Now she could sit on the couch in a T-shirt and leggings and feel comfortable. It was perfect. Others might laugh at her definition of perfection, but after the struggles of the past few years, to have someone come alongside and help them out was beyond anything she could have hoped for. So yes, it was perfect.

As she thought about the upcoming Christmas party, she knew it would make things even more perfect for Rachel. And because of that, she would do what she could to get them both to the party.

Rachel held tightly to Carissa's hand as they walked into the large ballroom. They'd arrived in a luxury car that Heather had arranged for them, and Rachel had been in awe of that. But that was nothing compared to the excitement on her face as she took in the beauty of the room they'd just entered.

Several Christmas trees loaded with decorations and lights filled the room. There were tables set up with cute signs announcing what they were. Some were for the kids to make decorations. Others were for decorating cookies. Chairs surrounded round tables covered in dark green tablecloths with centerpieces of white candles and red and white flowers.

At the far end of the room was a large chair next to the biggest Christmas tree in the room. Under the tree were tons of beautifully wrapped presents. Wandering around the room were people dressed in elf costumes, stopping to chat with the kids and helping them at the activity tables. Everywhere she looked, there was Christmas.

"This is amazing," Rachel said, her awe evident as her wide eyes looked around the room.

"Do you want to do something?" Carissa asked. "You could make a decoration for our tree, or you could decorate a cookie."

Rachel pressed close to her, grasping Carissa's hand in both of hers. "Will you go with me?"

"Of course, lovey."

"Then I want to make a decoration."

With that decision made, Carissa led her to one of the tables set up for making a decoration. She found an empty seat for her between a boy who looked younger than Rachel and a girl who looked about the same age.

There was an assortment of craft items for her to choose from, and one of the elves came to where Rachel sat. The young woman gave Carissa a smile, then bent to help Rachel get started on her decoration. Christmas music played in the background, but it wasn't loud enough to overwhelm the conversations taking place in the vast room.

Thankfully, neither of them stood out in their somewhat plain outfits. At a thrift shop, she'd found a pair of sparkly black leggings for Rachel and a red sweater that was a bit big on her but still looked cute. For herself, she just wore a pair of black pants and a green, long-sleeved turtleneck shirt. Carissa wished she could have dressed Rachel up in a cute Christmas dress, but that wasn't an option that year.

"Is she enjoying herself?"

The deep voice had her turning to see Hunter standing beside her. He wore a Christmas sweater that he didn't look entirely comfortable in, but it brought a smile to her face. He had his hands tucked in his pockets, and his gaze was on Rachel at the table.

"This is her first activity, but she definitely loves the decorations. Whoever you hired to decorate did a great job."

"Heather and my mom took care of all that. We had a fundraiser event recently, and the venue was decorated similarly, so I have a feeling they have someone they use for stuff like this."

"Thank you for inviting Rachel to this." She had already thanked Heather, but she felt like she needed to thank Hunter as well.

His gaze shifted to her, and a smile took his expression from stern to relaxed. She'd already noticed that he was a handsome man, but so far, she hadn't seen any real smiles from him in the few times they'd met. This smile, however, brought a warmth to his face that only served to increase his attractiveness.

"I'm glad that she's enjoying herself." His gaze returned to the table of children then moved back to Carissa. "How about you?"

"Oh." Carissa crossed her arms. "Well, I'm enjoying it too. Christmas is always a beautiful time of year, and Rachel simply loves it. Seeing her smile makes me happy."

"You do so much for her," Hunter observed.

Carissa couldn't argue against that statement. "Isn't that what parents are supposed to do? She's my world, and I'm all she has. If I don't do it for her, no one else will."

Hunter nodded. "My father was raised by a single mother, and from what he said, she did for him like you do for Rachel."

"All I want is for Rachel to grow up as happy as I can possibly make her."

"Mama, look!" Rachel turned around to show her the decoration she was working on. When she saw Hunter, her gaze widened, and she jumped up from the table. "Mr. King! Is this your party?"

Hunter smiled at her. "I suppose you could say it is. Are you having fun?"

Rachel nodded and held up her decoration. Hunter lowered himself to one knee, bringing them closer in height. He seemed totally interested as Rachel explained what she'd done.

Carissa wondered if he had any children himself. He didn't seem to have any problems relating to kids if his interactions with Rachel were anything to go by.

"I need to put more sprinkles on the star part," Rachel said as she turned back to her seat at the table.

Hunter straightened with a smile. "Is a trip to the cookie decorating table up next?"

"I think so, though she might want to explore the trees a bit. I think it's hard for her to only have a tiny tree to decorate at home. There's not enough room for all the decorations she'd like to put on it."

"Just make sure that you stick around for Santa. He's the best part of the party."

"I doubt that Rachel would let us leave before he made an appearance."

Hunter watched Rachel for a moment before smiling. "Smart girl."

"She definitely is." Carissa bit back the urge to share exactly *how* smart she was.

Carissa had no friends or family to whom she could brag about her daughter, and she deeply wished there was someone because Rachel deserved to be admired for her hard work and how seriously she took school. It was her hope that that determination would continue on throughout her life so that she never ended up in the same situation as Carissa.

"I guess I'd better keep circulating," Hunter said. "But I'm sure Heather will find you in a bit."

"Thank you again for the invite." Carissa hesitated. "And for everything else you've done as well."

Hunter seemed like he was going to say something but then just nodded with a ghost of a smile before he walked away.

She and Rachel had moved on to admiring the trees when Heather found them, an older woman at her side.

"Carissa," Heather said with a smile that looked an awful lot like her brother's, "I'm so glad you both could make it."

"Rachel is having a blast looking at the trees."

"They're all so beautiful," Rachel breathed with absolute adoration.

"Which one is your favorite?" the woman with Heather asked. "By the way, I'm Eliza King. Heather and Hunter's mom."

Carissa took the offered hand. "I'm Carissa, and this is my daughter, Rachel."

"It's a pleasure to meet you both." Eliza turned her attention to Rachel once again, also offering her hand to her. "So, do you have a favorite tree?"

Rachel shook her hand then said, "I like the silver one with the pink decorations. It's so pretty."

"It is *very* pretty," Eliza agreed. "Is pink your favorite color?"

"I do like it, but it's not my favorite. I like purple the best, but there aren't any purple trees here."

"Maybe next year I'll put in a special request that they include a purple tree for the people who like that color."

"That would be *awesome*," Rachel enthused. "I also like the red and white one with the candy canes because I love them. The peppermint ones, though, not the other weird flavors."

"I agree. Peppermint only."

Carissa glanced at Heather to see the woman watching her mother, a small smile on her face. She still wasn't sure what to make of this family and the things they'd done for her and Rachel. Eliza reminded her a bit of her own mom, and sadness swept in as she was reminded of all that Rachel had lost when Carissa's parents had been killed.

Both her parents had doted on Rachel, pouring on the love despite how she'd come to be in their lives. Now Rachel only had Carissa to love and cherish her.

There were days Carissa keenly felt her inability to provide Rachel with everything she wanted her to have. But she tried to keep in the forefront of her mind that her love was the most important thing she could give her. And now, with some help, she was able to give her warmth and a few extra Christmas memories.

CHAPTER 5

"She is absolutely adorable."

Hunter smiled as the two most important women in his life discussed Carissa and her daughter. He hoped that Carissa and Rachel were ready for a Christmas unlike anything they'd probably thought they'd have that year.

He knew it was just a matter of time before his mom suggested that they include the two in their family Christmas plans. At one time, their Christmas dinners regularly included people that his parents discovered had nowhere else to go. Since his father's death, however, that hadn't happened, but Hunter had a feeling it was all going to change that year.

His mother had gone through the motions of having the fundraisers and company Christmas parties over the past few years for the sake of their employees and the charities they supported. However, when it came to their personal holiday celebrations, it had been just their immediate family and George and his wife, Essie, who was also their housekeeper. Those two had been with them for as long as Hunter could remember and were part of the family.

Their recent Christmases had felt different...quieter...but they'd also been what the family had needed. Not having to assume a cheerfulness that none of them felt had been a welcome relief.

But now, for the first time since the accident, it felt like maybe they could eventually find their way back to a level of holiday cheer that his dad would have found acceptable. Probably not that year, but maybe it was time for a step in that direction. A step that might include a struggling single mom and her young daughter.

He was certain his father would have loved that.

"Do you mind if we extend an invitation to Carissa and Rachel for Christmas?" his mom asked.

"Why would I mind?"

His mom laid her hand on his arm. "I just wanted to be sure that you were comfortable with having someone else with us for Christmas once again."

"Hayden might have a problem with it, but I don't. Their need for a place to spend Christmas is greater than my need to grieve one more year." He gave her a smile. "I think it's what Dad would have wanted."

She blinked rapidly, her blue eyes tearing up for just a moment. "I think so too."

"Then yes, let's invite them." Hunter looked out across the large ballroom. "Now, whether or not Carissa will accept is another question."

"I think she will," Heather volunteered. "Especially if we make it mainly about Rachel."

Hunter glanced at his sister. "Well, it is mainly about her, isn't it? So that wouldn't exactly be a lie."

"Maybe it's about Rachel for Carissa," his mom began. "But for me, it's about helping a young single mom find a way to give her daughter the Christmas she no doubt wants to."

"I think I'm going to go see what they're up to." Heather glanced around. "Last I checked, they were at the cookie decorating table. I hope they've also been enjoying some of the food."

"I'm sure Carissa will make certain that Rachel gets some food to eat," Hunter said as his gaze swept the room in search of the woman. He found her easily enough, watching as she bent to speak to Rachel before straightening again.

Heather nodded. "No doubt."

"I'll speak to the caterers about packaging up some of the food to give to Carissa to take home."

Hunter watched as the women moved off in two different directions, leaving him to linger alone next to a large Christmas tree decorated with gingerbread men. His father had been much better about moving through the crowds, chatting with people, stopping to admire what the children were doing.

Emotion tightened his chest as he thought—yet again—about his dad, and he keenly felt the hole that his death had left in their hearts and lives.

"Excuse me, Mr. King." He turned to see a woman dressed up as Mrs. Claus standing beside him. "We're almost ready to have Santa Claus come out. Will you be giving a speech?"

Hunter nodded, trying to remember what he'd been rehearsing the night before in preparation for this moment.

"Okay," the woman said with a smile. "The mic is up on the stage next to Santa's chair. We've got everything organized. You just have to introduce the big guy."

Hunter followed her to the mic and waited as she introduced *him,* then took the mic from her when she was done.

"Welcome to our annual children's Christmas party," Hunter began as he looked out over the people who were gathered in the ballroom. "We're so glad to have you here with us today. As some of you may know, this was my dad's favorite time of the year, and this particular party was the highlight of his year. In his honor, we have continued having this party each Christmas. I hope you kids have had fun at the tables we've set up for you, but I'm sure you've been looking forward to this next part of the party. Who do you think has stopped by to visit us?"

Children's voices rose up all across the room, calling out Santa's name.

"Are you ready?" Hunter asked. Then over the hyper shrieks of excitement, he called for Santa to come out.

Santa Claus is Coming to Town played as the man they'd hired to play Santa came out onto the stage, waving and ho-ho-hoing loudly. If possible, the shrieks got even louder. Hunter found himself searching for Rachel to see her reaction, and he had to smile when he spotted her standing next to Carissa, her eyes wide as she clasped her hands beneath her chin.

The wonder and anticipation on her face, as well as on the faces of the other kids there, were why they had the party each year. Why they justified the expense when they could have just given the money to a charity. For a few hours, the children had the fun of decorating cookies, meeting Santa, and receiving a gift from him as well.

He handed the mic back to Mrs. Claus so she could explain the process of the children meeting Santa and receiving their gift. It had been a process that they'd worked out over the years to try and preserve the mystery of Santa, and it usually worked quite well.

His mom and Heather were up on the stage, helping to pass the gifts to the elves after matching numbers. Hunter kept an eye out for Rachel and Carissa, but they weren't in the line of kids. Frowning, he looked around, finally spotting them near the entrance to the ballroom.

Were they leaving?

Moving quickly, Hunter left the area by the stage and headed in their direction. Carissa was kneeling beside Rachel, her expression tense as she spoke with her.

"Are you ready to go up and see Santa, Rachel?" Hunter asked as he approached them.

Carissa looked up at him at the same time Rachel did. Their expressions couldn't have been more different. While Rachel's held an edge of stubborn determination, Carissa looked sadly resigned.

Rachel lifted her chin as she crossed her arms. "Yes, I am."

"Rachel," Carissa cautioned.

She turned to look at Carissa, her determination not wavering a bit. "I *have* to go, Mama. I need to tell him what I want for Christmas."

"You already sent him a letter."

"It's not the same. I want him to see me. I want him to see *you.*"

Carissa got to her feet. "Why does he need to see me?"

"He just does," Rachel said, and even though Carissa looked confused, Hunter knew why she was insisting on that.

"Visiting with Santa is part of the reason we have this party," Hunter told her. "It would be a shame if Rachel missed out on that." Carissa hesitated, and Hunter had a good idea of why. "Plus, I have it on good authority that Santa has a gift for *every* child here today."

When Carissa lifted a brow, obviously in query of that, Hunter nodded. "Why don't you come with me?"

At Carissa's nod, he placed his hand lightly on her back as he guided them to where the line had formed to see Santa. Since all the kids had already queued up, they were the last ones. As the kids finished with Santa, they returned to the tables scattered around the room, either to do more crafts or to eat.

The line moved pretty quickly, and Hunter stayed with them, holding a conversation with Rachel that included several attempts to get her to tell him what she planned to ask Santa for...as if he hadn't already read her letter.

"I can't tell you," Rachel insisted. "I haven't even told Mama. Only Santa is allowed to know. I hope he read my letter already."

"I think he probably has," Hunter assured her. "Santa mail is a priority at this time of year."

"Really?" Rachel's eyes went wide. "That is so cool!"

"It is, isn't it?" Hunter agreed, remembering back to when he'd been her age.

Carissa kept silent, but a smile played on her lips. He wondered what she'd think if she knew what Rachel was asking Santa for on her behalf. Something told him that she had more on her mind than trying to find a husband. It was entirely possible that the mother and daughter hadn't even discussed that idea.

As the line moved them closer, Rachel began to get more and more excited, dancing from one foot to the other, her hands clasped beneath her chin. The sight of her alternately made him want to smile and cry a little. It was hard to *not* smile at the anticipation and excitement on her face, but knowing that this was something that his dad would have enjoyed seeing immensely brought with it sadness and a fresh wave of grief.

Hunter hoped that soon he'd get to the point where it was mainly joy that came from thinking about his dad in relation to things like Rachel's excitement.

~*~

Carissa wondered if she could get close enough to Rachel and Santa to hear what she told him she wanted for Christmas. She really wanted to try to give her one thing she asked for that year.

"You stay there, Mama," Rachel said, pointing to a spot where other parents had waited.

So much for being able to hear anything. But rather than argue, she just went to the spot Rachel had indicated. Hunter, on the other hand, was allowed to approach Santa with her. He helped her up onto Santa's lap then stepped out of the way so the photographer could snap a picture or two. She hoped that somehow, she'd be able to get a copy of that.

Once the picture was taken, Rachel got down to business. Carissa recognized the intent look on her daughter's face, and she wished her phone was good enough to take a snap of the moment. Santa seemed to be taking his time with her, and Carissa supposed that might have been because Rachel was the last of the children to visit with him.

She noticed a slightly surprised look cross Santa's face, then he glanced up at Hunter before returning his attention to Rachel. Carissa's curiosity ratcheted up, but she knew it would be a curiosity that wouldn't be satisfied. At least not by Rachel. Maybe she could ask Hunter what he had heard.

Finally, Rachel gave Santa a broad grin then slid off his knee. Santa also smiled as Rachel headed to where Carissa waited, then he motioned for Hunter to approach him. Hunter bent down as the man began to speak to him, his gaze lifting from Rachel to meet Carissa's.

"Here you go, sweetie," a young woman dressed as an elf said, holding out a large gift bag with a picture of Santa and Mrs. Claus on it.

"For me?" Rachel asked, her eyes going wide.

"Yep. Merry Christmas!"

"What do you say, lovey?" Carissa prompted.

"Oh, thank you so much," Rachel said as she reached for the bag.

"You might need your mom to help you with it." The elf glanced up to smile at Carissa. "It's a bit heavy."

Carissa thanked her and took the handles of the bag. "Let's go sit at a table. Okay?"

Rachel nodded, her gaze on the bag. "Can I open it now, or do I have to wait for Christmas?"

Carissa would have liked to have her wait until Christmas so that she had something else to open then. But since she could see other kids opening their gifts right there in the ballroom, it seemed unfair to make her wait. "You can open it now."

"Thank you, Mama," Rachel said, skipping at her side as they walked to a table that was mainly empty.

Carissa hoped that she could talk Rachel into eating a bit more before they left, too, since it would mean she wouldn't need to feed her yet another bowl of vegetable soup that night.

Once at the table, Rachel perched on the edge of one of the chairs, an excited look on her face. Carissa put the bag on the floor in front of her then sat down on the chair next to her. Rachel eagerly opened the bag and pulled out the red and green tissue paper.

"Books, Mama," she breathed in awe. "Lots of books!"

Carissa leaned over to look inside, smiling at the realization that *books* must have been on her Christmas list—the one Heather had taken to mail to Santa. Rachel pulled out one of the books and squealed softly at the cover. "I haven't read this one yet!"

Rachel spent the next five minutes looking at each of the many books inside. Carissa put some food on a plate for them and tried to coax bites of it into Rachel's mouth between books. She didn't eat as much as Carissa had hoped she would, so she'd be having another bowl of soup that night.

"How's your gift, Rachel?"

Carissa looked up at Heather and saw that her mom was with her as well.

Rachel looked up from the book she was reading the back of and grinned. "It's perfect! Santa got my letter! I can't believe he really read my letter." She clutched the book she held to her chest. "I hope he can get the other things I asked for too."

Carissa gave her daughter a sharp look. She wasn't one for being greedy. "I think Santa bringing you this is wonderful, even if he doesn't bring you anything else on your list."

"I know, Mama. But it's not really something for me," she said. "I'm happy with my books. I don't need anything else."

Carissa glanced at Heather and her mother in time to see them exchange a look. It was a reminder that they were aware of what was on that list while she was being kept in the dark.

"We'll talk about it more at home, okay, lovey?"

Rachel nodded, then looked at Heather. "Thank you for inviting me to your party and letting me see Santa."

"You're very welcome," Heather said. "Are you going to decorate more cookies? Or make another decoration?"

The decoration was already tucked in Carissa's purse, along with the cookie that had been put in a small cellophane bag when Rachel had finished with it. The icing on it had probably smeared a bit, but Carissa wasn't sure that Rachel would care what it looked like when she ate it.

"Maybe one more cookie," Rachel said. "So Mama has one to eat as well."

"I think that would be a lovely idea," Heather's mom said. "You can do more than one, if you'd like. There are plenty of cookies available. Why don't we go see?"

Rachel gave Carissa a pleading look as the older woman held out her hand. "Can I go with her, Mama?"

Carissa knew that Rachel would be safe with Eliza, but it still took her a moment to nod her assent.

"My mom can't wait to have grandchildren." Carissa looked back at Heather, whose gaze was on her mom and Rachel. "Unfortunately, none of us are in a position to give her any, so she tends to adopt kids along the way. Hope you're okay with that."

How could she not be okay with it if it made Rachel smile? "Rachel doesn't have any grandparents."

Heather's brows lifted. "Really?"

"My parents have both passed away, and her father's parents...they didn't want anything to do with her when she was born."

"Very definitely their loss," Heather stated with a confidence that Carissa felt resonate within her. "Rachel is an absolutely charming child. You've done a wonderful job raising her."

"Can you tell me what was in her letter to Santa?" Her desperation to know had made her ask, even though she hadn't been sure that she should.

Surprise crossed Heather's face, then settled into an expression of consideration. "I'm afraid her requests are between her and Santa."

Carissa narrowed her eyes briefly. "And you as well, apparently. Those books are exactly something she would have asked for."

Heather smiled. "Santa is amazing, isn't he? Besides, I don't think you have to worry about her not getting everything she's asked for herself."

The peculiar phrasing made Carissa pause. "Did she ask for something for me?"

Heather's smile softened. "Like I said. You've done a wonderful job in raising her. She's a very thoughtful daughter."

"Oh, but I'm not worried about myself. I just wanted to make sure that I was able to get her something she wanted."

Heather lightly touched her arm. "You get her whatever you think she'd like and don't worry about the rest. It will be taken care of."

Carissa looked away, blinking back the moisture that pricked at her eyes. She wanted this to be a great Christmas for Rachel, and though it hurt to fall short on her own, she was so glad there were people who were willing to step into the gap.

"Thank you," she whispered, keeping her gaze lowered. She was truly grateful for their help, but there was shame in the whole situation for her too.

As if she could read her mind, Heather said, "There's no shame in accepting help when you need it. You are not alone."

And for the first time since her parents had passed away, Carissa found herself believing the words.

CHAPTER 6

Hunter had been making the rounds of the room once again, talking with more kids and their parents, when his gaze landed on Carissa and Heather. He couldn't help but be curious as to what they were talking about. Carissa stood in front of Heather, with her arms crossed and her head bent slightly.

He was pretty sure that Heather would never intentionally say anything to upset Carissa. But from where he stood, it appeared she was, indeed, upset about something. Without even thinking it over, he headed in their direction.

"Everything okay here?" Hunter asked as he joined them.

Carissa looked up at him, her eyes holding sadness that made his heart clench. He felt Heather grip his arm just above his elbow, pressing tight. He spared her a quick glance before turning his attention back to Carissa.

"It's fine," she murmured, her gaze lowered, fanning her dark eyelashes on her cheeks. "Everything's fine."

That response prompted another look at Heather. His sister just gave him a half-hearted smile even though she echoed Carissa's words. "Everything's fine."

Hunter didn't buy it for a minute, but Heather's reply meant he needed to back off. He wasn't going to get an explanation right then for what had transpired, but he would definitely get one from Heather when they were alone later.

"Look, Mama!" Rachel skipped up to them, a couple of cookies in her hands. His mom trailed behind the little girl, a smile on her face. "I made this snowflake for you."

Carissa bent over to look at the cookie that her daughter held. "It's absolutely beautiful, lovey. It's even sparkling like real snow."

"Yep! It's eat...able..." Rachel glanced at Hunter's mom.

"Edible glitter," she said, affection showing in the smile she aimed at Rachel.

"Yes." Rachel looked back at her mom. "The sparkle is eatable glitter."

"You did a good job with it. What's this other one?"

"It's a star. It's got the...eatable glitter on it too."

"I can see that. It's sparkling like a real star, isn't it?"

Hunter smiled as he watched the two of them together. Whatever Carissa had been feeling, she'd pushed it aside to interact with her daughter. His smile faded a bit as he realized that perhaps she had a lot of experience at pushing her thoughts and feelings aside so as not to have them spill over onto Rachel.

"Here is a box that you can put the cookies in," his mom said as she held it out to Carissa.

Hunter watched as Carissa helped Rachel slide the cookies carefully into the box. He had no idea how they kept the icing from smearing all over the place, but Rachel managed it, then Carissa closed the box and slipped it into the gift bag that sat on a chair next to her.

"I think we should probably head for home soon," Carissa said, running a hand over Rachel's hair.

"Did you get enough to eat?" his mom asked. "Actually, just wait here."

Motioning to Heather, the two of them headed in the direction of the caterers. Hunter had a feeling he knew what they were planning.

"So, did you open your gift from Santa?" Hunter said as he settled down onto one of the chairs at a nearby table so he was closer to Rachel's height.

"Yep. Mama said I could."

"That's good. Did you like it?"

"I *loved* it!" she exclaimed, her eyes sparkling with excitement. She flung her arms wide. "So. Many. Books!"

"Are they all books you haven't read yet?"

Rachel nodded. "I can't wait to read them all."

"I love books too," Hunter said.

Her little face lit up at his words. "You do? What books do you like?"

Hunter glanced at Carissa and found her watching him. "Uh. I kind of like scary-ish books."

"Oh..." The disappointment on Rachel's face was enough to almost make Hunter apologize for his choice of books. "I suppose that's okay. As long as they make you happy. Mama says I need to read books that make me happy."

"She's right, and I hope all the books Santa brought you do make you happy."

"Maybe I could let you read some of them after I'm done. I'd be happy to share."

Hunter felt his heart swell with affection for this little girl. Where was her father? Why wasn't he there, holding her hand, looking at her with the pride she deserved? Carissa might feel that she was lacking as a parent because she couldn't give Rachel things, but in his mind, she wasn't lacking at all. Rachel was a wonderful ray of sunshine.

"Thank you for being willing to share your books with me. How about you read them and then let me borrow the one you liked the best, and I'll read it."

Rachel looked up at Carissa. "Is that okay, Mama? Can I let him borrow my books?"

"Of course, lovey." Carissa ran her hand over Rachel's hair. "I'm happy that you want to share."

"Perfect," Hunter said. "Your mom can send me a message when you have a book for me."

Rachel beamed at his words. "It will probably be soon because every single one of these books will be my favorite. I just know it."

Hunter chuckled when Carissa admonished Rachel quietly. "I look forward to reading your books."

"You don't have to read them all," Carissa said. "I'll make sure she just gives you her absolute favorite."

"Don't worry about it," Hunter said. "I'm a pretty fast reader, so even if it's several books, I'll make the time."

Carissa stared at him for a moment, as if trying to figure out why he'd be interested in reading a little girl's books. Before she could say anything, his mom and Heather returned with a couple of bags.

"Here you go," his mom said as they set the bags down on the table. "These are leftovers from the caterer. Might as well not let the food go to waste."

Carissa frowned at the bags then looked up at his mom. From her expression, Hunter expected her to decline the food, but instead, she said, "Thank you so much. You've been so generous."

"You're very welcome, and you're doing us a favor taking it off our hands. It's mainly finger foods, but I thought Rachel might enjoy them."

"I'm certain she will," Carissa said as she gave Rachel an affectionate look.

"I'm so pleased that you both could make it today," his mom said. "We've really enjoyed having you here."

"And we've really enjoyed being here. I know Rachel has had a lot of fun, right, lovey?"

Rachel nodded enthusiastically, her curls dancing as she did. "It was perfect!"

"Are you able to stay for a bit, or are you heading out?" Heather asked Carissa.

Hunter glanced around and saw that a lot of the families were beginning to get ready to leave. Santa was the last official part of the party, so he wasn't surprised to see the room emptying out. Though he'd enjoyed the event more than he had in past years, Hunter was more than glad that it was drawing to a close.

"I think we should probably go home," Carissa said.

Hunter expected Rachel to protest, but she didn't, though her excitement seemed to dim slightly. However, she didn't say a word against her mother's decision to leave the party. He was just glad that they had a safe way to get home.

"I'll go ahead and let the driver know you're ready to go," Hunter said, pulling his phone out of his pocket. He texted a quick message to George, then waited for his response. "He'll be ready out front whenever you are."

"We need to get our coats," Carissa said, motioning to the coat check counter.

As a group, they moved in that direction, helping Carissa carry the additional items she'd ended up with.

Hunter went ahead and got his coat as well since he planned to walk them out to the car. His mom helped Rachel with her coat, then wrapped her worn scarf around her neck. The gloves Rachel pulled from her pocket were faded and had rips in the seams. Clearly, new boots weren't the only thing the little girl needed.

"Here, let me take those," Hunter said, reaching for the bags of food that his sister carried.

"Thank you again for your generosity," Carissa said once she had her coat on. "I really, really appreciate it."

"You're welcome," his mom said. "I'm glad you were able to come today."

Hunter was glad that his mom didn't try to brush aside Carissa's thanks. From their perspective in life, what they'd done for her that day really wasn't much. But he suspected that in Carissa and Rachel's eyes, it was a lot.

Once they'd said their goodbyes, Hunter went with them to the entrance of the hotel. He spotted the car right away and led them out into the cold afternoon air. George came around to meet them, a friendly smile of greeting on his face.

It didn't take long to get the bags situated in the trunk, then Carissa and Rachel got into the car. Hunter stepped into the space left by the open door then bent down to peer inside.

He looked first at Rachel. "Remember to let me know when you have a book for me to read."

"I will," Rachel said, giving him a broad grin. "I hope you'll like it."

"I'm sure I will." Hunter shifted his gaze to Carissa. "Please let me know if anything else goes wrong at the apartment."

Carissa nodded, though Hunter wasn't convinced she would. "Thank you again. For everything."

"You're welcome." He stepped back and closed the door, then stood watching as the car slowly pulled away from the front of the hotel.

As he watched the car merge into traffic then disappear around the corner, Hunter was left with an empty feeling in his chest, and he wondered how long it would be until he saw them again.

~*~

"Are you going to send Hunter a text?" Rachel asked. "He said I was supposed to let him know when I had a book for him to read."

Carissa looked up from her laptop to regard her daughter. "Are you sure that this book is your favorite?" Rachel nodded, her gaze serious. "You haven't even read all the books yet. How do you know this is your favorite?"

It wasn't that Carissa didn't want Rachel to give the book to Hunter. She just didn't want her to get her hopes up because she was sure that Hunter had better things to do than come to the apartment to pick up a book covered in pink hearts and unicorns. The only consolation, if there was one, was that if he intended to actually read the book, it wouldn't take him long.

"Mama, these books came from Santa, so *of course* they're all going to be my favorites."

"How many of the books have you read so far?" Carissa asked, setting aside her laptop. The discussion was actually a welcome break from what she was trying to do, which was to find an apartment in the area within her price range.

"Five."

Since they didn't have a television and Carissa had needed the laptop, Rachel had had time to fill. Thankfully, she'd had a stack of new books to spend time reading.

"Are you planning to give him all five, or do you have one favorite?"

"I'm going to let him see the books I've finished already, and he can pick which ones he wants to read."

Carissa sighed as she sank back against the couch. "Okay. I'll text him. Just know that he might be too busy to come by right away."

Rachel shrugged. "That's okay. Maybe I'll have even more books for him to look at when he comes."

Knowing she wasn't going to get out of texting Hunter, Carissa picked up her phone and found his number. She sat staring at the screen, trying to formulate the message.

Hi. This is Carissa, Rachel's mom. She has finished reading some of the books and has insisted that I let you know that she has some favorites for you to choose from. No rush! I'm sure you're busy.

Carissa read it over a couple of times before hitting send, then tucked her phone under a nearby cushion, trying to block the text and the man from her thoughts. She had other things that needed her focus, though she was discouraged enough to just give up for the night.

She'd been slowly increasing the area in which she was searching for an apartment, but if she moved much further away, Rachel would definitely need to change schools, and they'd need a new babysitter. Anxiety caused her stomach to knot, and she felt ill at the idea of all the changes that were coming.

Carissa didn't mind the changes for her, but the changes for Rachel weighed heavily on her. The sense of failing was keen as she stared at her laptop once again. Then, as if to add insult to injury, the screen went blank as the machine powered down on her.

She let out a frustrated sigh as she slid the laptop onto the coffee table. She had hoped to line up a few apartments to look at on Saturday. Because she had to work, she couldn't look at any during the week. Going in the evenings wasn't her first choice for various reasons, not the least of which was that it got dark so early. It just wasn't safe to be wandering around their neighborhood once that happened.

During the week, evenings were also a no-go because Rachel had school the next day, and usually she had at least a little bit of homework. That was why she'd been trying to line viewings up for Saturday or Sunday. Normally, she wouldn't have had much time on Sundays to look. But since her car had died and the bus didn't run near the church they usually attended, she had plenty of time.

Of course, now she'd have to wait and see if her laptop started up again. Last time, she hadn't been able to get it to start until the following day. The worst part was that she was paying money for the internet that they couldn't use half the time because of her laptop. She didn't have an internet-capable cell, or she would have just used it on the wi-fi.

When her text alert chimed, she fished her phone out, already knowing it would be Hunter responding. After all, she hadn't texted anyone else recently.

Hunter: *Actually, I can swing by in a bit. I'm just getting ready to leave the office. Is that convenient?*

She wasn't sure that any time would really be convenient when it came to her feelings where Hunter King was concerned. If she hadn't met the man, she would have definitely assumed he was an arrogant man just based on his position in life and his often-stern expression. Nothing was further from the truth, apparently.

The King family may have been one of the richest in the state—and maybe even the country—but they also appeared to be genuine and caring. It was a dangerous revelation, especially when combined with how wonderfully they'd treated Rachel.

That's fine. Rachel doesn't go to bed until eight-thirty.

Hunter: *Great. See you soon.*

As Carissa set her phone down, Rachel asked, "When is he going to come?"

"He'll be here in a little while. He's just leaving his office."

"Yay! Do you think Miss Heather will be with him?"

Carissa saw the hopeful expression on her daughter's face and felt a pang of...well, she wasn't sure exactly what it was. Or maybe she just didn't want to name it because it made her seem selfish. Still, it was hard to see her daughter so excited about the other woman when it seemed to be spurred on by what Heather had done for her.

Carissa could never compete with that. It was going to be a struggle to put even one present under the tree, but no doubt Heather and Hunter—and possibly their mom—would show up bearing a bunch of gifts for Rachel. She couldn't tell them not to come because then she would be saving her pride at Rachel's expense.

"I don't know, lovey. Maybe."

Carissa laid her pen and notepad down next to the laptop and got to her feet. In the kitchen, she put some water into a pot and turned on the burner. Her throat had been feeling a bit scratchy that day. They'd had a couple of employees at work who'd mentioned not feeling well earlier in the week, so Carissa hoped she hadn't picked up anything from them.

It was a bad time of year for sickness, in general. But her stress and anxiety were escalating, which meant she wasn't sleeping well, nor was she eating as well as she should have. Because of that, she was worried that she was going to come down with something. But more worrisome than that was the increased likelihood that Rachel would pick something up from Carissa if she got sick.

She found the bottle of lemon juice and the honey container she kept on hand, and when the water had boiled, she poured it into a mug before adding some lemon juice and honey. Rachel came over and watched her, her eyes wide.

When Carissa lifted the mug to take a sip, Rachel frowned. "Are you not feeling good, Mama?"

"I'm okay, lovey."

Rachel had had the lemon and honey drink before, so she knew what it was usually used for. "I hope you don't get sick."

"I hope so too." Carissa took another sip. "Have you got the books ready for Mr. Hunter?"

Rachel nodded. "Will he be here soon?"

"I imagine so. Have you finished your homework?"

"Yes. I put the math pages back in my folder. It's on the table."

Carissa continued to drink from her mug as she went to the table to review Rachel's work. She sat down on one of the chairs, feeling a weariness in her bones that seemed to be present more often than not these days.

When there was a knock on the door, Carissa looked up. Rachel ran to the door, but she didn't open it. Though they rarely had people at their door, they'd had plenty of discussions about safety and that Rachel should not open the door when Carissa wasn't with her.

Carissa moved Rachel behind her and left the chain in place as she opened the door, just to make sure it was Hunter. When she saw him standing there, she closed the door enough to remove the chain then stood back to let him in.

"Hi there," Hunter said as he walked into the apartment, carrying a couple of paper bags.

"Hey, Mr. Hunter," Rachel greeted him cheerfully. "I'm glad you came."

"Thank you." He gave her a warm smile. "I was told you had some books for me to borrow."

"Yes! A bunch of them, but you don't need to read them all."

"I hope it's okay that I brought some stuff for you two," Hunter said. "Can I set these on the table?"

"Uh, sure." Carissa led the way to the table, moving aside Rachel's folder and her mug.

"I hadn't had dinner yet, so I stopped along the way to pick something up. I figured that if you've eaten already, you can save this for tomorrow."

Carissa could smell the food, and her stomach growled in appreciation. It had been one of those days when Rachel had eaten most of their dinner. She'd come home from school starving, so Carissa had known that the little bit of food she'd prepared for supper would mainly be for Rachel.

Thankfully, Hunter was kind enough to not mention the noise her stomach had made as he opened the bags.

CHAPTER 7

Hunter had been surprised to receive a text from Carissa only a few days after the Christmas party. Although, as he thought about it while packing up some files to take home, maybe he shouldn't have been. Rachel had made no secret of the fact that she loved to read.

The stop for food had been an impulse when his stomach had growled once he was in the car. He was sort of inviting himself to stay for a bit longer. But he hoped that since he was bringing food for them, Carissa wouldn't get upset with him.

"I wasn't sure what you'd like, so I picked up a few different things." He reached into the first bag and began to pull out the food he'd ordered. "I got chicken strips, some soup, a couple of burgers, and a *bunch* of fries."

"Chicken strips?" Rachel appeared at his elbow and gazed up at him, her eyes wide. "I *love* chicken strips."

Hunter grinned down at her. "I thought you might. How about some fries? Does your mama let you eat those?"

"Yep! She does, but it's been *forever* since I had some."

He leaned down a little bit. "What does your mama like to eat?"

Rachel's brow furrowed. "I don't know." Her voice had dropped into a soft whisper. "She eats a lot of ramen, but I think that's because there's not always enough other food once she makes me eat."

"Rachel." Carissa's voice held a warning note, and when Hunter straightened and looked at her, she kept her gaze down, and there was a flush of pink on her cheeks. She was clearly embarrassed by her daughter's revelation.

"I also picked up a clubhouse sandwich and a chicken wrap." Hunter continued to pull food out of the bags. "So take your pick of anything."

"What are you having?" she asked, her voice soft.

"I think I'll have a burger," Hunter said. He'd had a craving for one, so he'd bought a couple, in case that was what Carissa or Rachel wanted as well. Carissa set some plates on the table. "You guys haven't eaten yet?"

"We did," Rachel said, her gaze on her mom as Carissa put a couple of chicken strips on one of the plates. "But there wasn't much to eat. I'm still hungry."

Hunter waited for Carissa to say something, but she didn't. She just put some fries on the plate then set it in front of one of the chairs. Rachel immediately slid onto the seat and smiled.

"Would you like something to drink?" Carissa asked.

"Water would be great."

Carissa went back to the kitchen then returned with glasses of water which she set in front of them.

"What did you want to eat?" Hunter asked as he looked at the array of food set out on the table.

"Um. I'll have the wrap. Thank you."

"You're welcome." Hunter set the wrap on one of the plates, then began to move the rest of the food—except for the fries—to the kitchen counter. The table was small, so there wasn't room for their plates and all the food he'd unpacked.

When he got back to the table, Carissa was helping Rachel open the packets of ketchup that had come with the fries. Once they were all seated, Rachel folded her hands.

"Should I say grace for this food, even though I prayed for what we ate before?" she asked. "Because I'm really thankful for these chicken strips and fries."

"Yes, lovey," Carissa said with a small smile, then gave Hunter a hesitant look before turning her attention back to Rachel. "Go ahead."

Hunter bowed his head and listened as Rachel recited a quick prayer, thanking God for the food. It made him smile to hear the sincerity in her voice as she prayed.

"And thank you for Mr. Hunter bringing us the food. In Jesus' name, amen."

Hunter murmured an *amen* of his own, then picked up his burger. He managed to hold back a moan as he took his first bite. He'd been busy all day and hadn't had anything to eat but a quick deli sandwich at lunch. His stomach was in heaven as he ate.

"How was your day?" Hunter asked after he'd taken a couple of bites.

No one responded at first. Carissa and Rachel looked at him, then at each other. "Go ahead, lovey."

"I had a good day," Rachel said as she swirled a fry through her ketchup. "Though the kids keep calling me a liar."

Hunter frowned. "Why's that?"

"Because I told them I met Santa and that he already brought me something that was on my list."

"Well, I'm sorry to hear that they thought you were lying," Hunter said. "But you know what? You know that you're telling the truth, and that's what's most important. If they don't want to believe you, that's their problem."

"I don't like it when they call me a liar, though, because I'm not."

"Yeah, it's not being very kind," Hunter agreed.

Rachel tilted her head as she lifted one of her chicken strips. "Have you ever had someone call you a liar?"

"Yeah. When I was younger sometimes. Now, as an adult, if they call me a liar, they don't do it to my face."

"Cause you could beat them up, right?"

"Rachel!" Carissa admonished as Hunter chuckled. "We don't beat people up."

"Well, yeah, Mama. *We* don't because we're not big, but Mr. Hunter is big. He could beat up people who call him a liar."

"It's true that I'm probably big enough and strong enough to beat someone up, but I wouldn't do that. Because even though them calling me a liar is wrong, so is beating someone up."

Rachel seemed to consider his words before nodding. "I just wish they wouldn't call me something that I'm not."

"Unfortunately, that's part of life, sweetheart. Sometimes it's best to just ignore people like that." Hunter turned his gaze to Carissa. "And how was your day?"

"It was fine. Nothing out of the ordinary."

"Where do you work?" Hunter asked, aware that she had a job, but not what or where that was.

Carissa finished chewing the bite she'd taken of her wrap, then met his gaze. "I waitress at a diner."

"Are you happy there?" Hunter realized as soon as the question was out of his mouth that perhaps it wasn't the most appropriate.

His dad had always said that if a person had a job they loved, they wouldn't feel like it was work. Of course, that didn't really take into account people who had to have a job to pay the bills, and who might not have the flexibility of switching jobs if they didn't like the one they had. He suspected that was the case for Carissa.

"I'm thankful for the job. My employers have been good about working with me on a schedule that accommodates my needs as far as Rachel is concerned."

"That's good."

"She still has to go to before and after school care, but it's not for too long."

"Do you like school, Rachel?"

Rachel nodded. "My teacher is nice, and most of the kids are too. Except for the ones who call me a liar." She tilted her head as she looked at him. "Did you like school?"

"I did, very much. My favorite subject was math. What's yours?"

"I like everything, but reading is my favorite. I want to be a teacher when I grow up," she said, then paused. "Or a nurse, like Mama."

Hunter glanced over at Carissa to find her frowning at Rachel. "You're a nurse?"

Carissa sighed then turned her attention back to him. "No. I was in nursing school when my parents died. They were my support, helping me take care of Rachel while I went to school."

"And when they passed away, you couldn't continue on?"

"I tried, but there was just too much happening. It was impossible for me to juggle everything."

Hunter lowered his burger. "How did they die?"

"They were in an accident," Rachel said when Carissa didn't reply right away.

"I don't know if you remember the horrible pile-up accident that occurred four years ago," Carissa finally said, her gaze on her plate. "Eleven people died. My parents were two of them."

A sick feeling invaded Hunter's stomach, robbing him of his appetite. "I do remember. My father was also one of those eleven."

"What?" Carissa stared at him, her eyes wide.

"My father was in one of the cars that the tanker hit. He died at the scene."

"I'm so sorry." Her shoulders slumped as her gaze dipped again. "My dad died in the hospital the day after the accident. My mom never regained consciousness, and she died a couple of days later. I didn't know who the other victims were. I was kind of caught up in my own bubble of grief, trying to adjust to living without them and all that meant."

Hunter nodded. "I understand that. We were in that bubble as well."

He could hardly believe how their lives had intersected in the past. His life, and those of his sister, brother, and mother, had changed irrevocably on that day, but they had still had each other. They'd still had their home. They'd still had the jobs they'd had before the accident. Jobs they'd been able to take time away from while they'd grieved without fear of losing them.

He hadn't even considered how others' lives might have changed as a result of the accident. He realized in that instant how self-centered he'd been. Yes, he'd been grieving, but he should have given some thought to others who had been impacted by the events of that horrible day. It would have been what his father wanted.

It may have been four years late, but at least he was getting to do something for one of the families impacted by what had happened. Even though they had already done some things for Carissa and Rachel, Hunter felt the urge to do even more.

And more than that, he wanted to make sure these two were in his life for as long as possible.

~*~

What appetite Carissa had, slipped away as she realized that their lives were tied together in a way she never could have imagined. It wasn't that she hadn't realized other people had been impacted by that accident. Eleven people were taken from the earth that day. Two of them were her parents, which left nine other people whose deaths had left gaping holes in the lives of their loved ones.

She set her wrap down, uncertain of what to say. Her hands shook a bit as she picked up her glass and took a sip of her water. "I'm sorry that you lost your father."

"Thank you," Hunter said, his voice low. "And I can't tell you how sorry I am to hear about your loss as well. I'm sure it's been an absolute nightmare for you."

It definitely had been. In the blink of an eye, her life had changed completely, and at that time, she'd only thought she'd have to adjust to the loss of her parents. It was only as she'd had to deal with everything afterward that things had really fallen apart for her and Rachel. She'd not been privy to her parents' financial situation, so it had been a shock to realize that their house had been remortgaged, and they had carried significant debt.

The financial situation she'd been left in had been strangling the life out of her. She'd had to sell what she could of her parents' possessions just to cover the cost of burying them. The house had gone into foreclosure, and she'd had to drop out of school, then scramble to get a full-time job plus an apartment that she could afford.

"Have you found an apartment yet?"

The question caught Carissa off-guard. Even though the feelings she was experiencing right then over finding an apartment were similar to the panic she'd felt four years ago, it took her a minute to switch gears. "Uh. Not yet, but I've been trying to view some."

"I'm sorry you have to deal with this right now," Hunter said.

"It's not your fault."

Hunter's brows lifted. "How do you figure that? After all, you have to move because I bought the building and made plans to demolish it."

"You gave plenty of advance notice about what was coming," Carissa said. "It's not your fault that some of us have struggled a bit more to get our act together. I'm not sure anyone would argue that this building shouldn't be knocked down. It's clearly not the safest place for people to live."

"True. That's why we made the plans we did."

"Why would you buy a building that just needed to be torn down?" Carissa asked.

"My dad always hated the run-down buildings, and each year, he would buy up a property in total disrepair and tear it down, then build a new building in its place. It wasn't his intention to do away with affordable housing for people who had limited incomes, but rather to try to offer them housing that was affordable *and* safe."

Carissa considered his words. "So you're building another apartment block here?"

He nodded. "This will be the third rebuild we've done in this part of town."

While she was glad to hear that the buildings weren't being torn down to accommodate luxury housing or a mall or something, it didn't help her with her current situation.

"We're trying to revitalize the area for lower-income families, not push them out."

She wanted to challenge him a bit on that because she doubted that the rent they'd charge on the new apartments would match what she and others in that block had been paying. It had been extremely hard to find a comparable place that she felt would be safe for her and Rachel.

But she kept her mouth shut. Like she'd said, her current situation wasn't necessarily his fault. She'd had a lot of time to find a new place, it just hadn't worked out like she'd hoped. Plus, he had gone over and above helping her when he'd realized that they had needed heat, hot water, and a better way to cook. Not to mention another month rent-free.

"Are there many suitable vacancies in the area?" Hunter asked as he picked up his burger again.

"Not too many." Not *any*, if she wanted to be totally honest, but she didn't really want him to know how dire their situation was.

He seemed to sense that perhaps she wasn't completely honest with him since he gave her a searching look. But apparently, he decided not to push her because he dropped the subject.

"Can I have more ketchup, Mama?" Rachel's question helped diffuse part of the tension that had built up in Carissa during the conversation.

She gave Rachel some ketchup, then picked up her wrap. Hunter had turned his attention back to Rachel, asking her more questions about the books she'd been reading.

Carissa wasn't sure how she felt about the sudden involvement of others in their lives. For the past four years, with the exception of the babysitter and a neighbor or two, they'd had very few people get close to them. Even the people at the church they attended weren't more than passing acquaintances. No one had come into their lives to the extent that Hunter and his family recently had.

She was quite certain that she and Rachel had become their charity case for the season, and if it wasn't for how their help benefited Rachel, she would have protested. Rachel didn't understand the dynamics of charity and pride, and that was fine by Carissa. If she had to swallow her pride so that Rachel had the memory of this special Christmas, then she'd do just that.

"Do you have a wife, Mr. Hunter?" Rachel asked.

"Oh." Hunter glanced over at Carissa, then back at Rachel. "No, I don't. And Heather doesn't have a husband either."

"Do you have any kids?"

Carissa went to silence Rachel, but then Hunter answered her. "Nope. No kids either."

"Do you *like* kids?"

"Well, sure, I do. Kids are great. I mean, I was one once, so I should know. And I especially loved being a kid at Christmas time."

Rachel nodded. "It's my favorite time too. We're going to go to the holiday parade. Right, Mama?"

"Yes. If it's not too cold." Carissa tried to find things for them to enjoy during the Christmas season that didn't cost money. The parade was one of those things, and she usually took a little money along to buy a treat for Rachel while they were there.

"I haven't done that in years," Hunter said. "I hope it's warm enough for you to go and enjoy it."

"You should come with us," Rachel said. "You and Miss Heather. I bet you'd have a lot of fun."

"I'd have to talk to Heather first."

Carissa figured that there would be a point where they wouldn't be interested in being involved with them any further. She couldn't blame them for that, and maybe wandering around in the cold would be where they drew the line. It wasn't her first choice either, but she had a good reason to do it.

"We didn't go last year because it was too cold, but I've been asking God every night in my prayers to make it so it's not so cold this year. I really want to go."

"Well, I'll pray too," Hunter said, his expression serious, as if he really was going to pray about the weather for a Christmas parade.

Though they usually went to church each Sunday, Carissa sometimes felt like she went more for Rachel's sake than her own. She still wasn't sure how she felt about God after what had happened with her parents. She'd struggled a lot with anger towards both God and her parents in the year following the accident.

She was well aware that bad things happened, even to people who trusted in God. It had already been so hard to lose her parents. She could have done without the financial mess she'd had to deal with after their deaths. She'd just wanted to be able to grieve the horrible loss she'd experienced. But instead, she'd had to deal with bills and the foreclosure. The financial stress on top of the grieving had been unbearable.

So while she wanted Rachel to continue to grow her childlike faith, Carissa had struggled to grow in her own faith. She never discouraged Rachel from praying about anything, and her trust was inspiring.

"I'll let you know if it will work for Heather and me to come," Hunter said.

Rachel leaned closer to Hunter, looking up at him with wide eyes. "I really hope you can make it."

"We'll try, sweetheart."

The endearment appeared to roll off Hunter's tongue, and he didn't even seem to notice what he'd said. Carissa noticed, though, and Rachel's eyes grew wider—if that was even possible—but Carissa wasn't sure if that was because he'd said they'd try to come or because he'd used such an endearing nickname.

Seeing Rachel interact with a man like Hunter reminded her of all Rachel had lost when her grandparents had passed away. Given the fact that Rachel's father had signed away his parental rights as soon as she'd been born, Carissa's father had been the only significant male influence in Rachel's life. Thankfully, he'd happily stepped into that role. But with his death, Rachel's world had narrowed down to just her and Carissa.

While she was glad that Hunter was so good with her, it worried Carissa a bit. She didn't want Rachel to get too used to him being in their lives. Once Christmas was over and they had moved to another apartment block, she had a feeling they wouldn't be seeing him or Heather again.

And Carissa wasn't going to even think about how it felt for her to have Hunter around, to be reminded of what it was like to not shoulder the responsibility of a child's happiness all on her own. Still, sitting there at the table with the two of them, she couldn't help but think how nice it was and how much she appreciated his willingness to interact with Rachel. Not every man would have an interest in doing that.

CHAPTER 8

"I can't believe you convinced me to do this," Heather said as she looped her scarf around her neck.

Hunter laughed. "Like it took all that much convincing. You were on board right from the moment I suggested it."

"That was before I realized how cold it was going to be." They left the warmth of their mom's home—which was also where Heather lived—and headed for the waiting car. It was one of their larger SUVs since it needed to comfortably seat the four of them plus the driver.

Once in the warmth of the vehicle, Hunter sat back, not bothering to voice to his sister that he was a little surprised that he'd told Rachel they'd go to the parade. But there had been no way to resist the pleading in her wide eyes.

Plus, he found he liked doing things that made the little girl smile because that inevitably made her mom smile. And Carissa and Rachel's smiles, he'd decided, were well worth enduring a little cold for.

George, their driver, headed down the long driveway then out onto the street. Hopefully it wouldn't take them too long to get to Carissa's and then to where the parade events were being held.

When they pulled up to the run-down apartment building, Hunter got out and headed to the front door. He was reminded once again of the lack of security as he walked straight in. Climbing the steps in the dim light was another reminder of the deterioration of the building.

When he knocked, the apartment door didn't open right away, but he heard Rachel's muffled voice through the door telling Carissa someone was at the door. As she had on each of his previous visits, Carissa opened the door with the chain in place first, then once she saw it was him, she released the chain and opened the door more fully.

"We're just putting on our coats," she explained with a wave to Rachel, whose head was bent as she focused on getting her zipper done up.

Hunter looked at the worn jacket and knit cap the child wore and hoped that she'd be warm enough. His gaze dropped to her boots, remembering the letter to Santa where she'd asked for new boots because the ones she had hurt her toes.

"I'm so excited!" Rachel exclaimed as she tugged her mitts on. "And I'm so glad you and Miss Heather could come to."

Hunter said, "We're excited too."

Maybe not as much as Rachel was, but that was to be expected since they were adults, after all.

It didn't take them too long to get out the door, but as Hunter glanced over at Carissa, he wondered if they should be going at all. She looked tired...more tired than he'd seen her before...and she'd coughed a couple of times into her elbow like she was getting sick.

Out at the car, he saw that Heather had moved to the back seat. Rachel quickly climbed in to sit next to her, eagerly talking about what she hoped to see that evening. Hunter waited for Carissa to climb in and settle in her seat before closing the door and going around to get in on the other side.

"Thank you for picking us up," Carissa said, her voice soft. "I usually take the bus with her, but this is so much easier."

Hunter struggled with the urge to make everything easier for Carissa. It was within his power, after all. Excessive wealth made things like that fairly simple, but he had to weigh that urge to assist against her pride. So far, he figured she'd accepted their help because of Rachel. But there would probably come a point where she'd feel they were taking over her life, and Hunter didn't want that to happen.

"And I made it even easier by bringing George," he said, gesturing to the man in the driver's seat. "Saves having to find a parking spot when there are so many people."

Hunter looked over at Carissa as George drove away from her building. She had a knit cap on as well as a scarf, so he hoped she'd be warm enough. Though she faced away from him, he heard her muffled cough and wondered again if she was getting sick.

From the back, he could hear Rachel telling Heather about the book she was reading. He had to smile at her excitement. He'd read a couple of the books she'd given him, and while they were definitely not something he'd choose of his own accord, he could see why they'd appeal to a young girl in a big way.

He wanted to talk to Carissa, but she seemed wrapped up in her own thoughts. Or maybe it was just the tiredness he'd sensed from her when she'd opened the door earlier.

When they reached the part of the city where the Christmas events were being held, the driver pulled over to let them out. The sights and sounds of Christmas greeted them, as well as a crowd of people. It was the first night of the event that would run mainly on the weekends from that night until Christmas.

"Hey, Mr. Hunter," Rachel said as she tugged at his sleeve. "We're staying for the fireworks, right?"

"As long as it's okay with your mom."

"Mama?" Rachel slid her hand into her mom's and looked up at Carissa. "Can we stay?"

"Of course, lovey."

"Let's go have a look around then," Heather said. "See what kind of trouble we can get into."

Rachel abandoned Carissa to walk ahead with Heather, the two of them no doubt conspiring what all they were going to do for the few hours they would be there.

"Are we gonna eat here?" Rachel asked, glancing back over her shoulder.

"We already ate, lovey," Carissa said, her voice holding an edge of reproof.

"But I'm still hungry, and it smells so good."

"Let's look around and see what they have," Hunter suggested, certain that the main reason Carissa was objecting to getting food there was because of the cost.

There was a reasonably good selection of stuff with a nice balance between sweet and savory. They ended up at a BBQ food stand, where they each managed to find something to eat. Hunter wasn't sure that Rachel would be happy with anything from there, but it seemed that she wasn't a fussy eater. That and the promise of mini donuts seemed to do the trick.

Carissa tried to pay for their food, but Hunter insisted. "Just let me take care of this, okay?"

She peered up at him for a moment before nodding, a resigned expression on her face. Hunter almost felt guilty for covering the cost of things like that because it was clear that it bothered her. But that guilt lost out to the desire to give her and Rachel a nice evening out.

They found a place to sit down, and after Rachel said a prayer for the food, they all dug in. Hunter was happy to see Rachel clearly appreciating her food. Carissa ate more slowly but seemed to be enjoying it as well. Hunter was definitely on board with what they'd picked up for dinner. It was tasty and warm, and since he'd only had a sandwich for lunch, it satiated his hunger.

"Hayden said he might show up," Heather said as they ate. "Depending on how he's feeling."

"Who's Hayden?" Rachel asked as she looked up from her food.

"He's our brother," Heather said.

Rachel's eyes went wide. "You have two brothers?"

"I do. Hunter and Hayden."

"Is he nice like you guys?"

"Usually," Heather said with a smile.

"Oooh. I would love to meet him."

"You might get to," she told the little girl. "He doesn't always feel like getting out, but he thought he might make an exception for tonight."

"I think he'd have a lot of fun," Rachel announced.

Hunter hoped that was the case if Hayden showed up. There were days when he didn't even leave his room. He'd been in the car with his dad that fateful day, and the trauma of the accident along with the overwhelming number of physical injuries he'd sustained had left Hayden struggling daily, both physically and mentally.

"Are you guys almost done?" Rachel asked. "I want to go look around."

"Be patient," Carissa said. "We'll be ready to go in a bit."

Hunter wondered if Rachel was going to argue, and for a moment, it looked like she was gearing up for that. But instead, her shoulders slumped as she nodded. "Yes, Mama."

Carissa slipped an arm around her shoulders and kissed her knit cap-covered head. "Thanks, lovey."

Hunter didn't dawdle over his food since he understood the young girl's eagerness to see what all was there. When Heather got a text from Hayden saying he was on his way, Hunter went to meet the car that was bringing him while Heather and Carissa cleaned up their food.

"Good to see you, buddy," Hunter said as Hayden climbed from the back of the SUV. He was using crutches, and the tension on his face told Hunter that his brother wasn't having a good day. It made him wonder why Hayden had agreed to join them.

"Good to see you too." Hayden gave him a one-armed hug before stepping back, using his crutches to keep his balance. "Thanks for letting me tag along."

"Oh, you're in for a real treat," Hunter said. "Rachel is super sweet, and so is Carissa."

"Yeah. Mom said they were nice."

"What made you decide to come out?" Hunter asked.

Hayden gave a huff of laughter as they slowly made their way to where Hunter had left the others. "My therapist said I needed to make an effort to get out this week. I see her tomorrow, and I hadn't gone out yet."

"Ah. Well, I'm glad you decided to bless us with your company." Hayden gave a snort. "I hope you don't regret it."

"That makes two of us," Hayden said as he bumped his shoulder into Hunter's.

~*~

Carissa helped Heather clear up all the stuff from their dinner. Rachel helped a little, but her attention was clearly captured by everything going on around them. The food had been filling, and she would have appreciated it more if she wasn't feeling so yuck.

Her chest felt tight and heavy, and her throat was scratchy. And if she wasn't mistaken, she was running a fever.

She tugged her scarf up over her mouth when the urge to cough came again. Walking to the garbage can, she lifted her elbow and coughed into it. Hopefully, they wouldn't be out too late because she wanted to go to bed early that night.

She had an appointment to look at an apartment the following day and wanted to not be too exhausted to go. She had hoped to spend time looking at more, but she was just too tired.

Maybe, just maybe, she'd experience a miracle, and it would be as good as the ad said for the price. She wasn't holding her breath, however. Too many hopes had been dashed lately. It was easier to not have hope anymore.

"Mr. Hunter's back," Rachel announced.

Carissa looked over to see Hunter approaching with a man who looked almost identical to him. Unlike Hunter, however, this man walked with the use of crutches, and as they got closer, she could see that he also had scars on his face.

"Hi," Heather said, giving the man a hug. "So glad you could come out tonight."

"Just trying to appease a therapist," he said, his voice low.

"Whatever the reason, I'm glad you're here," she said, then turned toward Carissa and Rachel. "Hayden, this is Carissa and her daughter, Rachel."

"Why do you have to use those?" Rachel asked before Carissa had a chance to greet the man.

"Rachel." Carissa felt a flush of embarrassment over Rachel's question as she turned her attention to Hayden. "I'm so sorry." She held out her hand. "It's a pleasure to meet you."

"Please don't worry about it," Hayden said, giving her hand a firm shake. He looked down at Rachel and gave her a smile that only lifted one side of his mouth. "I have to use them because I hurt my leg in an accident. They help me to keep my balance, especially on the ice."

Rachel nodded. "That would be bad if you fell. I've fell on the ice, and it hurt my bum."

"Definitely not fun."

"I like the crutches. They look cool."

"Hunter got them for me," Hayden said.

"That's so nice you got them for him, Mr. Hunter," Rachel said with a grin in Hunter's direction.

"I thought it was nice of me too."

Hayden elbowed Hunter in the ribs. "And so humble too."

"Why do you look so much like Mr. Hunter?"

Hunter laughed. "I guess we didn't tell you yet that Heather, Hayden, and I are triplets."

"Triplets? What are those?"

"It means we were all born at the same time," Heather explained.

"You have the same birthday?"

"We do," Hunter said. "But the really interesting thing is that Hayden and I are actually identical twins. Heather was just the tagalong."

That explained why they looked so much alike, Carissa mused as she glanced between the brothers. And even though Heather was no more genetically like them than any other sibling would be, she still looked very similar to both men as well. She very much looked like a female version of them since they all shared the same color of hair and eyes.

"Can we get some mini donuts and walk around?" Rachel asked, apparently done with the sibling discussion.

Carissa sighed. She knew Rachel was excited, but her manners didn't have to go out the window.

"I would like that too," Heather said. "I'm still kind of full, though. But hopefully, walking around will help me make room for mini donuts."

With that, their little group set off with Heather and Rachel in the lead. Carissa fell into step beside Hunter while Hayden walked on Hunter's other side. There were lots of things to see, and lots of people there to see it all. Sometimes it was slow going as their group maneuvered around other groups. They weren't going fast anyway because Hayden moved slower with his crutches, and Carissa was fine with that because she just wasn't feeling that great.

They moved as a group through the crowds of people there, and Carissa forced herself to ignore the aches in her bones and the tightness in her chest. She wasn't surprised that she was sick. With everything going on lately, she was run down physically and emotionally, which inevitably would lead to her getting sick.

"You doing okay?" Hunter's voice had Carissa lifting her head to look at him. "You look like you're someplace else."

"I'm sorry," she said.

Hunter shook his head. "Don't apologize. I just wanted to make sure you're doing okay." A rueful look crossed his face. "Though I realize as I say that, I know that you've got a lot going on, so it's very likely that you're not doing okay."

Carissa couldn't help but appreciate his acknowledgment of her situation, even though it didn't change anything. He'd already done so much for them. More than he really needed to. His only responsibility to them had been to give them reasonable notice before the building was going to be demolished. And he'd done that. It wasn't his fault she hadn't managed to find a new place for them to live yet.

"Mama!" Rachel skipped to her side in a way that had Carissa holding her breath, waiting for her to wipe out on the slippery surface of the sidewalk.

"What's up?" she asked.

"Can we have hot chocolate?"

Carissa thought of the small number of bills she'd shoved into her pocket earlier, planning to use the money to pay for their meal. Since Hunter had covered that, she still had that money. The practical side of her wanted to say no to Rachel and keep the money to buy a few more groceries. But the side that wanted to do things that brought joy to Rachel's life had her agreeing.

"I suppose so," Carissa said with a smile at Rachel. "Have you seen a place where we can get some?"

"Over there." Rachel pointed with a mittened hand to a small food truck that boasted not just hot chocolate but mini donuts.

Bracing herself for the inevitable, Carissa took her hand then turned to Hunter. "We'll be right back."

"Actually, I think hot chocolate sounds like a great idea," Hunter said. "I'll come with you."

Before long, all of them were headed in the direction of the food truck. There was a bit of a line-up, but it seemed to be moving fairly quickly. No surprise, Hunter pulled out his wallet and paid for all of them. Carissa tried to protest, but once again, he brushed aside her attempts to pay.

Given everything Hunter and Heather had already done for them, Carissa didn't want them to think that she was taking advantage of them. She knew that she'd never be able to repay them for everything. What puzzled her the most was why they had done anything for her and Rachel beyond making the apartment livable.

"Here's your hot chocolate, Little Miss," Hunter said as he handed a small disposable cup to Rachel.

Carissa couldn't help but smile at the Little Miss reference, though she wasn't sure that Hunter got the humor of it. Would he have ever made his own hot chocolate from little packets of powder?

Though the others had gotten hot chocolate, Carissa had decided to get some hot apple cider in hopes that it would help soothe her throat. The first sip felt glorious, and she hummed in appreciation.

As they moved away from the food truck, she wasn't sure where they were headed, but Heather and Rachel were in the lead and apparently had a plan. Hunter and Hayden were talking as they fell in step together behind the other two. Hayden's pace was slow, which Carissa appreciated as she brought up the rear, sipping at her cider.

Though she was feeling physically terrible, a bit of joy swirled around inside her. It wasn't something she'd thought she'd experience much of that year, with everything that weighed down on her, but somehow it was there. She knew, though, that the people who had delivered the things that had contributed to the joy were but vessels. For whatever reason, God had chosen to send them their way.

She still had to find a place to live. Her car was still doing a remarkable impression of a rock. And right then, she felt horrible. But despite all of that, she chose gratitude—she was so very grateful—and she chose joy.

As she watched the brothers in front of her, she could see that Hunter had adjusted his steps to match his brother's. It spoke to the caring nature of the man, as did all the things he'd done for her and Rachel.

It would be so easy to fall for the man. She hadn't made the best choices of men earlier in her life, but something told her that Hunter wouldn't be another bad choice.

Unfortunately, she wasn't a good choice for someone like him. A single mother barely able to provide the necessities for her daughter. Hunter needed someone more like his sister. Confident, beautiful, and engaging. All things that Carissa didn't feel she was. At least not in recent years.

As her joy began to drain away at those thoughts, she frowned and pushed them away. It wasn't the time to reflect on how not good she was. She could do that later that night as she struggled to find a home for her daughter.

"Carissa?" Hunter said, looking around before coming to a stop. He turned back, relief on his face when he spotted her. "I thought we'd lost you."

"Not much chance of that. I can see you two even in a crowd."

"Well, come walk with us," he said, holding his hand out toward her.

Carissa didn't take it—she was sure that wasn't why he'd held it out—but she did fall into step beside him, spotting Rachel and Heather not that far ahead of them.

"You doing okay?" he asked.

"I'm fine." The hot cider had helped a bit, but she'd probably be drinking more hot lemon and honey when she got home.

"I'm glad that Rachel suggested this," he said. "I'm really enjoying it."

"I've brought her a couple times. It used to be a tradition with my parents to go to something like this each year."

"Traditions are nice, but they're also hard when the person or people who were part of the tradition are gone." Hunter paused, then said, "That children's Christmas party was my dad's idea, and he was usually Santa. It gave him so much joy to interact with all the kids like that."

"It looked like it gave the kids there a lot of joy to interact with Santa and do the other activities you had for them. I'm sure I'm not the only parent who is glad you've continued to host the party even though it's probably not easy for you."

"It's what Dad would have wanted. He loved kids." Hunter smiled. "He would have loved Rachel."

"Would he have read books with unicorns and hearts on their covers?" she asked.

Hunter chuckled. "Oh, I think he definitely would have. If it was something that would put a smile on a kid's face, he'd do it."

"He shouldn't have died," Hayden said, his voice rough. "The world was robbed."

Pain laced Hayden's words, and Carissa felt it echo inside her. The world had been robbed of eleven lives that night. The anger she felt about what she'd had to deal with after her parents' death faded for a moment, leaving only grief behind. She'd been robbed. Rachel had been robbed. Death had robbed them all of people they should have had in their lives for years to come.

How did one move past that grief?

Carissa didn't know, but she hoped that it happened soon. She wanted to just remember the good times with her parents. She didn't want the grief and anger anymore.

CHAPTER 9

Hunter pushed back from the desk and went to the large window that looked out over the city, unable to focus on the files he needed to review. He'd come in on a Saturday to try and catch up on some work that he hadn't been able to finish the previous day. He wasn't accomplishing much, though.

Instead of reviewing the files, all he could see were the faces of Carissa and Rachel the night before. Rachel's had seemed to absolutely glow throughout the whole evening. That had made the outing even better. The event hadn't really been his cup of tea—or coffee, as it were—but being there with Carissa and Rachel had made it fun and enjoyable.

Carissa had been quiet most of the evening, leaving him to chat with Hayden until the evening had become too much for him, and he'd called for a car to take him home. Even then, she'd stayed quiet, mostly reacting to Rachel, indulging her frequently. Hunter was glad that he wasn't the only one who felt like giving the little girl the world.

But now, he wanted to give Carissa the world too.

He turned from the window and stared at the box that sat on the couch on the other side of the room. He'd had the guys in his IT department find the best laptop available which would hopefully meet all of Carissa's computer needs. Not that he knew exactly what she did with her laptop. But from what Rachel had told Santa, they used it for watching videos, so he wanted it to at least be more than good enough for that.

He was pretty sure that Carissa was going to protest the gift. But he'd let her know that it was from Santa at Rachel's request.

Even as he planned gifts for the pair with his mom and Heather, he knew that what Carissa needed more than anything was a new apartment. And that was something he was going to help her with as well, even though she'd probably get upset with him.

A couple of apartments had become available in a building the company owned not far from the on where Carissa currently lived. He planned to offer it to her, and if she fought him on it, he'd just encourage her to view it as a short-term solution, even though she'd be welcome to stay there as long as she wanted.

It was his hope that it would take some of the pressure off of her during the holiday season, and then she could resume looking in the new year when the weather was nicer if she still wanted to move.

The urge was strong to just try to move the two of them into a much nicer apartment and cover the cost himself, but he knew that wouldn't be what Carissa wanted. Though she'd allowed them to do a lot of things already, in the big scheme of things, they'd been relatively small and had been focused on Rachel.

The fact that Carissa didn't let her pride get in the way of providing for her daughter was an attractive quality for Hunter. He'd heard plenty of stories from his dad about the sacrifices his mom had made to provide for him. No doubt she'd had to swallow her pride at times, much like Carissa had done in the past couple of weeks.

But an apartment? A permanent place for her and Rachel to live paid for by him?

No. He had a feeling that would be a step too far.

So he would do the next best thing. Find an apartment in one of the buildings the family owned that was close to the area where they lived now. They'd have to find some middle ground on the rent since she wouldn't believe it was the same as where she currently lived. Leaving Carissa with no options was unacceptable, and he knew that if his father was alive, he'd agree.

He returned to his desk and pulled up the options that Stan had emailed him regarding available apartments. There were two that could possibly work. That he had the hope of a chance of talking Carissa into considering.

Picking up his phone, he tapped the screen to call her. It rang a few times before going to voicemail. Frowning, he tapped it again.

This time it was answered with a tentative, "Hello?"

"Rachel?" Alarm grew within him as he considered all the reasons why she'd be answering her mom's phone.

"Who's this?"

"It's Hunter, sweetheart. Can I talk to your mom?"

"She's sleeping," she said. "She's sick."

Hunter began the process of shutting down his computer. "How long has she been sleeping?"

"A long time. I'm hungry."

Trying to quell his worry, Hunter put his Bluetooth earpiece into his ear, then grabbed his jacket and pulled it on. "I'm on my way to your place now. I'll bring you something to eat."

"Thank you," she said.

Rather than make her worry more about her mom by asking her lots of questions, Hunter tried to get her to talk about her books as he left his office for the basement parking garage, jogging where he could to get there as fast as possible. He kept talking to her as he got into his car and pulled out of the parking garage.

"Rachel, sweetheart, are you close to your mom?" he asked at one point.

"I'm sitting next to her in bed. I don't want to leave her."

"Good girl. Can you put your hand on your mom's forehead for me?"

"She's really, really hot."

"Thank you, sweetheart. You just hang on. I'll be there in a few minutes." He didn't want to get off the phone with Rachel, but he suspected they would need an ambulance.

When he pulled to a stop at a red light, he took the opportunity to send a quick text to Heather.

On the phone with Rachel. Seems Carissa is unresponsive and hot to the touch. On my way there now. Will call with an update when I get there. Might need help with Rachel.

"Are you still there, Mr. Hunter?" Rachel asked, her voice more timid than he'd ever heard it.

"I am, sweetheart. I was just sending a message to Heather to let her know I'm going to visit you."

"Okay. I'm glad you're coming." She gave a little sniff. "I'm worried. Mama's never like this."

"She's going to be just fine," he said, hoping he wasn't lying. "And you're such a good girl for staying by your mom like that. And just so you know, if you're ever worried about your mom like this, you can always call me or Heather, okay?"

"Okay."

Hunter was glad that his office wasn't too far away, but it still felt like it took him an eternity to get there. When their gray block of a building came into sight, he breathed a sigh of relief.

There was no parking available right in front of the building, so he had to go past it a little. Once he was parked, he shut his SUV off and climbed out.

"Rachel, I'm at your building now. I'll be upstairs in a couple of minutes," Hunter said as he jogged toward the entrance. "Can you come to the door and let me in?"

"Yes."

He took the stairs two at a time, hoping he'd manage to miss any weak spots. The last thing they needed was for him to injure himself while trying to help Carissa and Rachel.

He tried to catch his breath as he reached the door. "I'm here."

He heard locks disengaging, and slowly the door opened to reveal Rachel. Her hair looked like it hadn't been brushed yet that day, and he barely got a glimpse of her worried expression before she threw herself at him.

Scooping her up in his arms, he held her tight. "Everything's going to be okay, sweetheart."

He shut the door behind him, then moved down the hallway to the bedroom. He hoped that Carissa would forgive him for barging in on her, but this definitely classed as an emergency.

His text alert dinged, but he ignored it as he went down on his knees beside the bed. Carissa's forehead was as hot as Rachel had said, and her face was flushed, and her lips looked dry and cracked. At a guess, Hunter figured she was dehydrated, possibly from having to fight such a high fever.

"Carissa?" He touched her shoulder, which was covered by a sweatshirt, then gently shook her. "Carissa?"

She gave a low moan and then winced. "Rachel?"

The word was raspy and barely above a whisper.

"She's here. She's fine," Hunter assured her.

As he looked from Rachel's worried face to Carissa's still form, Hunter made a decision that he was sure that Carissa would object to, but he had no medical experience. She needed more help than he could provide for her.

Settling on the floor, he drew Rachel into his lap as he placed a call to 911, then gave the operator the details as he knew them.

When he hung up, Rachel said, "Is she going to die?"

"No." There was no other answer that Hunter was willing to consider at that point. "But she's sick, so we need her to go to the hospital so they can give her the medicine to make her better."

"What about me?"

Hunter looked down at her. "What do you mean?"

"Do I stay here and wait for Mama by myself?"

"No. You'll come with me to the hospital. You'll stay with Heather or me until your mom is feeling better. Is that okay?"

She nodded, her hands pressed against her lips as she watched her mom.

"You're very brave. I'm proud of you, and I know your mom will be too."

He checked the text message and saw that it was from Heather.

Heather: *What do you need me to do?*

Meet me at the hospital. I've called 911. She has a really high fever, and I think she's dehydrated. Not sure what to do for her.

The message was a bit disjointed, but Hunter knew that Heather would understand.

He heard the distant sound of sirens, so he helped Rachel stand up then got to his feet. With her hand in his, he made his way to the front door and opened it.

There was a flurry of activity as the EMTs arrived and went right into the bedroom, asking questions of Hunter as they assessed the situation. As Hunter had hoped, they decided the best place for Carissa was at the hospital.

Rachel stood pressed against his leg, his hand gripped in both of hers, as the EMTs took Carissa out on the stretcher. If he'd been able to handle getting her to the hospital on his own, he would have tried to spare Rachel that sight. But there was no way he would have been able to get Carissa down to his car on his own. At least not safely.

"Okay, sweetheart, let's go."

"I'm in my pajamas," she said, gesturing to the all-in-one outfit she wore.

"That's okay. We'll get you some clothes later."

She hesitated but then nodded. Hunter helped her put her jacket and boots on, then grabbed the booster seat by the door. All the way down the stairs and as he drove to the hospital, Hunter prayed that Carissa would recover quickly from whatever sickness she had.

He also kicked himself for not canceling their plans the night before when he'd gotten the sense that she wasn't feeling well. If only he'd forced the issue.

~*~

Carissa woke to the feeling of knives jabbing into her throat and a tightness in her chest. "Rachel?" As the realization dawned that she wasn't in her bedroom, panic began to rise. "Rachel?"

"Hey, hey. She's fine."

Shifting her gaze, she blinked, and Hunter came into focus. "Where is she?"

She wanted to ask more, but the pain in her throat stopped her.

"Heather's taken her to the cafeteria. You're in the hospital."

"Why?"

Hunter's brows rose. "You weren't responding because of a high fever, and you were dehydrated."

"How?"

"I phoned you, and Rachel answered. She told me that you were sleeping and wouldn't wake up. I was concerned so came over and decided to call 911."

She glanced around the room. "Go home?"

Hunter shook his head. "Not yet. They're giving you an IV for the dehydration and also to get some antibiotics into you." When she frowned, he continued on, "You've got a chest infection and strep throat."

She'd had strep throat before, but it had never put her in the hospital. Granted, it hadn't been when her body was so run down nor when she'd also had a chest infection. Given that she had a bit of medical experience because of the year of nursing school she'd had, she should have known better.

Thinking that she'd need to spend the day in bed, she'd told Rachel that she could eat any of the food in the fridge if she woke up before Carissa. She'd also given her permission to sit on the bed next to her to watch her favorite shows. Carissa knew she had a fever, but since she didn't have medicine to bring it down—there was only children's medicine in the cabinet—she'd hoped that it would just run its course.

Clearly, she'd been a fool. What would have happened if Hunter hadn't come into their lives? What would have happened to Rachel, left alone with Carissa feverish and unable to communicate?

Panic gripped her, making her stomach heave, even though there was nothing in it. Swallowing against the urge to vomit sent shafts of pain through her throat.

"Hey, you're okay. Rachel's okay." Hunter took her hand in his, and Carissa clung to it. "Everything's going to be fine."

She closed her eyes as she tried to take breaths, feeling very much like nothing was going to be fine. Nothing was going to be okay.

"Everything okay here?" a woman asked.

Carissa kept her eyes squeezed shut as hot tears slid across her face.

"Is it possible to get something for her pain? And maybe something to drink?"

"Let me just check her over really quickly, and then I'll see what I can do about that."

Carissa opened her eyes when prompted to by the nurse, then gave one-word answers to her questions. Hunter had stepped back, but he hadn't left the small room.

The panic eased a bit, but it wasn't completely gone. What was going to happen to Rachel while she was in the hospital? She felt the gaping hole in her life left by her parents' death more keenly than ever.

"Mama?" Rachel appeared beside her bed and grabbed her hand. "Are you okay, Mama?"

Carissa nodded. "Love you."

Rachel pressed her cheek to Carissa's hand. "Love you too, Mama."

Carissa ran a hand over her hair, so glad she was okay but worried about what would happen next.

Hunter moved to stand behind Rachel, resting a hand on her shoulder. "Don't worry about Rachel, okay? My mom is preparing a room for her as we speak, and then when you're discharged, you'll go to our place as well."

Carissa frowned, then tried to force more words past her sore throat. "You don't have to do that."

"Maybe we don't have to, but we want to," Hunter said. "Right, Heather?"

Heather nodded without hesitation. "We have plenty of room at the house, and we'd love to have you stay with us. We were going to ask you to come for Christmas anyway, so this is just a little in advance of that."

"I don't want to be an inconvenience."

"You're not. In fact, you'll give Mom something to do. She gets bored so easily."

Carissa had a hard time believing that. From the little she'd seen of the woman, she didn't appear to be one who just waited around for something to do.

"If you feel strongly about going back to your place when you get out, we can talk about it again," Hunter said, causing Heather to turn and stare at him.

Though she figured that he was just saying that, Carissa appreciated that he was at least pretending that she would have some say in what happened. Or maybe he'd just realized that she'd capitulate simply for Rachel's sake.

She gave a single nod, then turned her attention back to Rachel. Hunter helped her up onto the bed, where she snuggled into Carissa's side. Heather moved a wheeled table closer to them, then set a bag and a drink on it.

"We got some apple juice and a sandwich for Rachel," Heather said as she opened the bag. "And a donut for Hunter."

"No coffee?" he asked as he took the small bag Heather held out.

"So demanding," she said with a shake of her head. "I'm pretty sure you've drunk plenty already today."

Heather opened the apple juice, and Rachel sat forward to take it from her.

"Do you want some, Mama?"

Carissa quickly shook her head. She was thirsty, but sharing a cup didn't seem like the smartest thing. As it was, she would have to keep an eye on Rachel to make sure she didn't come down with anything.

Hunter left the room, presumably searching for coffee, while Heather stayed with the two of them. Rachel worked her way through the ham and cheese sandwich, not complaining about it not being peanut butter and jelly. Carissa hoped that she'd eaten some of the food in the house because the idea of Rachel being hungry made her heart hurt.

She was grateful that Hunter had tried to call them that day, though she had no idea why he would have. It was hard to accept that she couldn't do everything by herself, but it was clear that she couldn't. Just because her self-sufficiency had worked up until the last few days didn't mean that something like this wouldn't happen again.

For Rachel's sake, she needed to open herself up to friendship more than she had. Maybe she could find another single mother who, like her, needed support, so they could be that for each other.

Hunter reappeared after about ten minutes with two coffees and another bag in his hand. "Here you go, sis." Heather took the cup he handed her. "And look what I brought for Rachel."

He set his cup on the table and opened the bag. Pulling out a large cookie, he smiled as he held it out to her. "Don't tell your mom."

Rachel gave a laugh as she looked up at Carissa. "Close your eyes, Mama."

Happy to play along with anything that made Rachel laugh right then, Carissa closed her eyes. It actually felt good to block out the light, and she had to fight to not relax back on the pillows and fall asleep. She wondered how long they'd keep her in the hospital.

"Do you want a bite, Mama?"

Opening her eyes, she looked down at Rachel and gave her a smile while shaking her head. "It's for you."

"It's yummy. It has chocolate chips."

"I thought you might like chocolate," Hunter said.

"I do."

"Say thank you, lovey," Carissa said, trying not to wince at the pain in her throat as she spoke.

"Thank you, Mr. Hunter and Miss Heather."

"You're very welcome."

"I would have brought you something," Hunter said, "but I wasn't sure what your throat might handle."

"I'm fine." Even though she hadn't eaten anything since the night before, she wasn't very hungry. Certainly not hungry enough to force anything past the painful inflammation in her throat. In fact, she even wished that she didn't have to swallow her own saliva.

Hunter settled into a chair against the wall, sipping at his coffee as Rachel chattered on about the books she'd been reading. When Heather's phone rang, she left the room to answer it.

A few minutes later, she came back in. "Are you okay here, Hunter? I'm going to head home."

"Yep. I'm good. I'll bring Rachel to Mom's in a little while."

Hunter appeared to be in no rush to leave, but Carissa knew it would probably be better for Rachel not to hang around the hospital too long. She had a sick feeling in her stomach at the idea of being separated from her daughter.

Part of her wondered if she was too trusting of Hunter and Heather. But did she have any choice? Rachel couldn't stay with her in the hospital.

She wished that she could ask the babysitter to take her for the night, but the woman's home was small with barely enough room for her own family.

Was the painful connection she shared with the King family, along with all they'd done to help her and Rachel, reason enough to trust them? Carissa hoped so because she couldn't risk coming to the attention of family services. She didn't think they'd take Rachel away from her right away. But between her not having anyone to care for Rachel if she wasn't able to and the current state of their home, they would definitely draw some attention.

She prayed that she wasn't making a mistake. That what she'd seen from the King family was a true reflection of who they all were. They may have had a shared tragedy in their past, but that didn't automatically mean they were good people.

Except she really felt that they were. Hopefully that was an accurate feeling and not something based on wishful thinking. Rachel's life could depend on it.

Nurses continued to come in and out, checking on her. Though Carissa still felt awful, she also felt like she was taking up a bed that she didn't really need. But as long as she was attached to an IV, she wouldn't have much choice, and she knew that it was important that she get liquids and antibiotics into her.

"We should probably head to my mom's," Hunter said as she began to doze. "Are you still okay with that?"

After a brief hesitation, she nodded.

"I know you're worried," he said. "All I can give you is my word that Rachel will be safe. You can call me or Heather at any time to video chat with Rachel. Even if you just need to see her sleeping, you can call either of us."

"You live there too?" Carissa asked, trying to keep her voice soft and not strain it.

"No, but I'm going to stay there tonight to help with Rachel."

"Okay. But she doesn't have any clothes and stuff with her, does she?"

"Don't worry about that. Mom and Heather got things for her for tonight. Pajamas. Toothbrush. That sort of stuff. Does she have a routine that we should know about?"

Carissa nodded. "Bath. Pjs. Teeth. Story. Prayers. Bed."

"I should be taking notes." Hunter pulled out his phone, then repeated it back as he typed it out. "Any type of snack?"

"Snack!" Rachel said with a grin.

Carissa smiled at Rachel, then said, "Just for tonight, any snack is okay."

"Thanks, Mama," Rachel exclaimed.

"You be good for Mr. Hunter and Miss Heather, okay?"

Rachel nodded, but then her brow furrowed. "But why can't I stay here with you?"

"Not in the hospital, lovey. Just for tonight, you stay with them."

It seemed to dawn on her then that she was going to be without Carissa for the night. Carissa braced herself for some waterworks, and she knew if that happened, she'd probably start crying as well.

Hunter knelt down beside Rachel. "Do you like dogs?"

Rachel nodded. "I want a dog, but Mama says not right now."

"Well, my mom has a dog named Chloe. She's an older dog, so not very energetic. But if you sit and pet her, she'll love you forever."

"Chloe? I love that name, and I think I'll love her too."

"Why don't you say goodnight to your mama, then we'll go see Chloe. We'll come back here right after breakfast tomorrow, okay?"

Hunter lifted Rachel onto the bed, and Carissa fought back tears as she hugged Rachel tightly. When she sat back, Carissa cupped her cheeks and pressed a kiss to her forehead.

"Be good, lovey. I love you."

"Love you too, Mama."

Rachel kissed her cheek then climbed off the bed with Hunter's help.

"If your throat starts to hurt, you tell Mr. Hunter, okay?"

"I'll keep an eye on her for that," Hunter assured her. "I want to say try not to worry, but I know that's probably impossible. Just concentrate on getting better. We'll see you tomorrow bright and early."

Carissa wasn't convinced she would sleep at all that night. But not long after Hunter and Rachel had left, she found herself drifting off.

CHAPTER 10

Hunter cupped his hands around the mug of coffee that sat on the counter in front of him. Grateful that Essie had taken one look at him and made the coffee a bit stronger than usual, he lifted the mug and took a sip.

The previous evening had been a bit of a challenge because once Rachel had stopped being enamored by the dog, she'd gotten scared and weepy. He couldn't blame her for that because from what he'd picked up, she had never been away from her mom for the night before.

And then there was her reluctance to sleep alone. At first, they'd thought maybe having Chloe on the bed with her would be enough, but unfortunately, that hadn't been the case. It wasn't until Heather agreed to sleep with her that she'd finally settled down and fallen asleep.

Neither of them had appeared yet that morning, but they'd left the bedroom door open a crack so that she would feel comfortable leaving the room if she woke up before Heather did.

In the meantime, he was trying to kickstart his brain with some caffeine while Essie, the family housekeeper, started on breakfast.

Esther—better known as Essie—had been with their family for thirty years, starting when she'd been hired in her mid-twenties. She had fallen in love with George, who had originally been hired as a handyman/caretaker of the property, though he'd gone on to become their driver as well. They'd gotten married shortly after meeting each other, and Hunter couldn't remember a time when the couple hadn't been part of their life. They were family now, living in their own spacious suite above the garage.

"More coffee, darling?" Essie asked as she turned on the stove burner and set a pan on it. Before he could even formulate a response, she was heading in his direction with the coffee carafe.

"Thanks, Essie," he said as she topped off his mug. "One more, and I should actually be alert."

"I hear we have a little one visiting."

"Yep. The daughter of a friend."

"Why is she staying here?"

"Carissa is a single mom, and she ended up in hospital overnight. She didn't have anyone else to care for Rachel, so we said we'd take her for the night."

"Is she a close friend?"

The question caught Hunter off-guard, and in the time it took him to answer, Essie's smile began to grow. "It's not like that."

Though to be honest, he kind of wished that it was. Pushing that thought out of his mind for the time being, Hunter told Essie the story of how they'd come to be involved in the lives of Carissa and Rachel. He hadn't told his mom yet about the tragic connection they shared, but he did tell Essie.

She listened as she continued to make breakfast. "It's just terrible that they were living in those conditions. Do they have somewhere new to move to?"

Hunter still felt a bit guilty for that, despite doing everything they could to give the people in that building the time and extra funds to find a new place. "Not yet. But I plan to make sure they have a home soon. She'll be coming here first, though, until she's fully recovered and able to take care of Rachel on her own."

"That sounds like an excellent plan," Essie said. "Maybe they should just move in here. It would be nice to have a little one around."

"I'm not sure Carissa would want that. She seems to be very independent."

"Sometimes people are independent by nature. Other times, they are independent because they have no choice but to be that way."

Hunter pondered that for a moment, then nodded. "I can't say for sure which one it is for Carissa. But I know for certain that she would do anything for her daughter."

"Well, at least she has a support system now. Although that will only work if she takes advantage of it."

"Which she may not," Hunter said. "She's been managing everything on her own for several years. I'm not sure she'll change overnight."

"You just have to keep reminding her." Essie set a plate of pancakes and bacon in front of him, then handed him the syrup. "Eventually, she'll figure out that you're there for her and Rachel with no strings attached."

Hunter didn't want to attach strings to his help, but he couldn't help but hope for a chance to tie their lives together more closely.

After he poured syrup on his pancakes, he bowed his head and said a prayer for the food and for Carissa as well. He wasn't sure if he should take Rachel with him to the hospital or if it would just be easier to go by himself and bring Carissa back, assuming she would be discharged.

Carissa would definitely want to see Rachel. But a cold front was rolling in, and it would probably be easier to not drag her out in such nasty weather. Before he could come to a decision, Heather and Rachel walked into the kitchen.

"I smell bacon!" Heather exclaimed as she came to the table. She settled Rachel on a chair then went to greet Essie. "Good morning, Essie."

"Morning, sweetheart. Do you want eggs? Or are pancakes okay with your bacon?"

"Pancakes and bacon are fine." Heather walked back to the table and sat down next to Rachel. "Do you want pancakes and bacon too?"

Rachel's eyes went big. "Both of them?"

"Yep. You can eat as much as you want," Hunter said. "I'm having both."

Rachel looked at his plate and grinned. "I want both too."

Essie quickly brought over two plates of food for Heather and Rachel. "There you go. Eat up."

When Rachel folded her hands and closed her eyes, Hunter exchanged a look with Heather and then bowed his head again, listening as she thanked God for her food and then asked Him to take care of her mom at the hospital.

"I'm going to go pick up your mom soon," Hunter said as he lifted his mug then took a sip of coffee.

"Can I go with you?" Rachel asked.

"Sure, but it's freezing outside. I'm just going to go and pick her up and come right back here." Providing nothing bad had happened through the night. And if something *had* happened, it might be better if Rachel wasn't there.

"Why don't you go by yourself," Heather suggested. "But if you end up needing Rachel there, I'll bring her. Just leave George to drive me. I don't want to have to hassle finding a parking space and then walking Rachel through the cold."

Hunter nodded. "Okay, that sounds like a plan."

They kept eating, and Hunter was glad to see Rachel enjoying her breakfast. It gave him a glimpse of what Christmas morning might be like if she was still around—and Hunter very much wanted her to be there. And her mom, too.

Once he finished his breakfast, he got up, prepared to head to the hospital right away. He knew that Carissa would be worried about Rachel and, provided the doctors released her, would want to leave the hospital as soon as possible.

"You promise to bring Mama home?" Rachel asked as he carried his dishes to the sink.

"I promise, or if she has to stay a bit longer, I promise you can come to see her." He bent over and pressed a kiss to the top of her head. "Heather, Essie, and my mom will take care of you until we get back."

"Okay. Tell Mama that I love her."

"I will, sweetheart."

His mom walked in then and greeted them all. She sat down at the table with Heather and Rachel. "Have you eaten, Hunter?"

"Yep. I'm just off to the hospital to get Carissa, hopefully."

"Oh, I hope they discharge her. I look forward to having her here with Rachel."

Essie brought a plate of food and set it in front of his mom.

"Thank you, Essie," his mom said. "This looks delicious."

"Can we save some for Mama?" Rachel asked. "I think she'd like pancakes and bacon too."

"I will make sure to save some for her," Essie said as she smiled at Rachel. "Would you like some more?"

While they sorted out what more Rachel wanted to eat, Hunter said goodbye and headed for his vehicle, stopping to talk briefly with George to let him know the tentative plans for the hospital run.

Since it was Sunday morning, the traffic wasn't too bad, and he made it to the hospital in good time.

When he stepped into Carissa's room a short time later, he saw that she was sitting up and looked rested.

"Hey there," he said. "How're you feeling?"

"Better," she said, her voice still soft.

"Did you sleep okay?" She nodded. "And how's your throat and chest?"

"Still sore, but better than it was."

Hunter was glad to hear that. "I left Rachel with Heather because it's really cold out there. But if you'd like her to come, I can let Heather know to bring her."

"Did she have a good night?"

"She had a bit of a struggle falling asleep. But once Heather agreed to sleep with her, she settled right down."

Carissa grimaced. "I'm sorry. She's used to sleeping with me."

"It was not a problem. When I left, Mom, Heather, and Rachel were enjoying a breakfast of pancakes and bacon. Rachel made sure that we saved some for you because she figured that you'd like some."

"You didn't need to save any for me."

"Believe me, it's not a problem. There's plenty of food. Essie always makes a lot."

"Essie?" Carissa asked.

"My mom's housekeeper."

Carissa's eyes widened briefly, but before she could comment on that, a nurse and doctor entered the room. Hunter offered to leave, but Carissa told him to stay. Stepping back out of the way, he listened as the doctor talked with Carissa.

Thankfully, it sounded like the doctor was going to release her. Hunter hadn't thought they'd keep her in longer now that the dehydration had been dealt with and they'd gotten some antibiotics into her.

"You ready to get this show on the road?" Hunter asked once the doctor had signed the necessary papers to release her from the hospital.

Carissa nodded. "I need to change."

Hunter realized then that she only had the clothes she'd been wearing when the EMTs had brought her to the hospital. "Are you okay wearing the stuff you had on last night? I'll give you my jacket to wear outside."

"You don't have to do that," Carissa protested softly.

"It's not a problem. I have a thick sweater underneath."

She was still frowning as he stepped out of the room so she could change. When she was done, she came out of the room, ready to go. But before then, they also had to make a stop to fill a prescription for antibiotics.

Moving slowly, they made their way down to the entrance.

"I'm going to go get the car, so wait here, and then I'll give you my jacket." Carissa hesitated, then nodded. "I'll be right back."

A blast of cold greeted him as he stepped from the building. He pressed his remote car starter, then jogged to where he'd parked the SUV earlier and climbed behind the wheel, cranking the heat so that hopefully it would warm up a bit before Carissa got in.

When he pulled to a stop in front of the entrance, he left the vehicle parked and running as he quickly went to get Carissa, taking off his jacket as he walked.

"Are you sure it's okay for me to wear it?" she said. "I don't want you to be cold."

"I'll be fine."

His jacket swamped her, but it would keep her warm. Once she had the jacket on, he led her to the SUV and opened the passenger door. Carissa didn't hesitate to climb into the seat.

After he slid behind the wheel, Hunter adjusted the vents so that most of the heat was directed to Carissa. Given the nature of her illness, he didn't want to take the chance on making things worse for her when it seemed like maybe she was finally doing better.

He realized that she needed some clothes and toiletries if she was going to stay at his mom's. Maybe Heather was up to buying some clothes for her. Or maybe they'd have to make a trip to the apartment and get stuff for both Rachel and Carissa.

Though he knew it was probably unlikely, he hoped that Carissa would be willing to stay at his mom's through Christmas, which was only a week away. After all, they'd already talked about including the pair in their Christmas celebrations, so having them there for a few extra days wouldn't be a big problem. And he was quite sure that his mom would love having them.

So would he, for that matter.

~*~

Carissa stared in awe at the house situated at the end of the driveway that Hunter had turned into. It was a huge brick home with lots of windows and a large front door. She had never been in a house of that size, but it looked like that was going to change.

Hunter pulled around the circular driveway and came to a stop at a spot closest to the front door. He'd barely stopped when the front door opened, revealing Rachel and an older woman she recognized as Hunter's mother.

Without waiting for Hunter to get out, Carissa unlatched her seatbelt and opened the car door. She moved along the interlocking brick sidewalk as fast as the lingering weakness in her body would allow, then climbed the steps and opened her arms to embrace Rachel. She was so relieved to see that her decision to let Rachel go with Hunter and Heather hadn't been the wrong one.

"Come on inside, you two," Eliza said. "It's too cold to hang out on the porch."

Carissa followed Rachel into the foyer, trying to resist the urge to stare at everything. In a quick glance, she did manage to see a considerable number of Christmas decorations spread throughout the foyer. She took off Hunter's jacket and handed it to him as he stepped into the house.

"Thank you for letting me use it," she said.

He gave her a warm smile. "You're very welcome."

"Why don't you bring your mom in here, sweetheart," Hunter's mom suggested to Rachel.

"We saved you some pancakes and bacon, Mama."

"Is that what you had for breakfast, lovey?" Carissa asked as she allowed Rachel to lead her into the kitchen. She was very aware of the fact that she was wearing her pajamas which consisted of a pair of flannel pants and a sweatshirt.

"I did! And they were nummy. I wanted to make sure you had some too."

"Thank you, lovey. That was very sweet of you."

As they walked into a large kitchen, she spotted another middle-aged woman there. Hunter's mom introduced her as Essie.

The woman greeted her with a friendly smile. "Why don't you sit yourself down, and I'll bring you the pancakes and bacon that Rachel insisted we save for you."

Rachel still had hold of her hand and pulled her over to a breakfast nook that sat in an alcove with large windows that looked out over an expansive, snow-covered backyard. "Sit, Mama."

Carissa didn't fight her daughter's command since she was feeling the need to sit down anyway. She hoped that she could do justice to the food that the woman put in front of her.

Essie must have seen something in her expression because she patted her shoulder lightly and said, "Just eat what you can. I know bacon's not an easy food to eat with a sore throat."

"Thank you very much."

"You're welcome. We're so happy to have the two of you here."

Carissa had a hard time believing that, but she appreciated the woman's attempt to make her feel comfortable. Plus, she was going to try her best to enjoy the bacon since it had been quite awhile since she'd last had some.

Hunter and his mom appeared a moment later and settled at the table with her and Rachel, each accepting mugs of coffee from Essie with words of thanks. Hunter held out the little container of pills they'd stopped to pick up.

"Do you need to take a pill now?" he asked.

"I think so," she said, taking the bottle from him. As she dumped a pill out into her palm, Essie set a container of yogurt next to her plate.

When she looked up at her, the woman said, "If you're on antibiotics, it can be a good idea to eat yogurt."

Carissa nodded, happy to eat it, not just because of the probiotic benefit it would give her but also because it would be easy to swallow considering her sore throat.

"Are you feeling better?" Eliza asked after Carissa had bowed her head to say a prayer of thanks for the food and everything that Hunter and his family had done for them.

"I am. I didn't think it would get as bad as it did."

"I guess things like that can take a turn for the worse quite quickly," Hunter said.

Carissa still had a tremendous amount of guilt over the fact that Rachel had been alone while she had been feverish and basically unconscious. It scared her to think of what could have happened if Hunter hadn't called that day.

"Everything's fine," Hunter said gently, reaching out to cover her hand for a moment. "Don't think about the what-ifs."

She nodded, but that was going to be easier said than done. It was just one more thing to add to the list in her head of how she'd failed her daughter.

"I hope that you are okay spending some time with us," Hunter's mom said as Carissa began to take small bites of pancake and bacon, chewing as much as possible so that it wouldn't hurt when she swallowed. "We'd love to have you stay through Christmas, even if you're feeling better before then."

"You want us to stay with you for Christmas?" Carissa asked.

"We do," the older woman said with a smile. "It would be so wonderful to have a little one around to make it a more exciting time for all of us. These older three have outgrown stockings and Santa."

The woman made it seem like Carissa would be doing them a favor by staying, but she couldn't really understand that. Still, the idea of giving Rachel the type of Christmas that likely happened in that huge, beautifully decorated house was tempting. Oh, so tempting.

"It would be great if you could stay," Hunter said.

"I need to go to work," she said, glad that she hadn't missed any days at work yet.

Hunter frowned. "Do you have any sick or vacation days?"

"A couple, maybe," she told him.

"I think you're going to need to take at least Monday and Tuesday off."

Carissa wanted to argue with him, but she knew that he was right. It wouldn't be a good idea to go to work until she was feeling much better. "I'll call them today to let them know I need a couple of days off, but I think I still need to work the rest of the week."

This time it was Hunter that looked like he wanted to argue, but he didn't. "Is Rachel done at school?"

Carissa nodded. "Tuesday is her last day of school."

"Can she miss a couple of days?" Hunter asked.

"I suppose so. I don't think they do too much other than fun stuff for those two days."

"Okay. So why don't you continue to stay here, and Essie and Mom can watch Rachel for you while you go back to work?"

It was an idea that strongly appealed to Carissa, especially since she doubted that the women would take payment for watching Rachel. It would save her some money because she would have had to pay the babysitter extra to keep her all day.

But she didn't want to take advantage of them.

They must have sensed she was on the verge of refusing because Hunter and Eliza went into high gear to convince her to stay. Rachel and Essie both joined in.

Because of the added pressure, Carissa knew that she was going to give in. Not for herself—though she had to admit that the prospect of spending time with friendly, kind people, good food, and a warm, comfortable home had certainly not hurt. But this was her one chance to give Rachel a truly memorable Christmas, which she hadn't been sure she'd be able to do considering how the year had gone.

She was thankful for the people who were stepping into the gap to help her and Rachel at what was one of the lowest points of their lives. Losing her parents had been low. Finding out how bad the financial situation had been had dragged them lower. But this year, with her car breaking down, their apartment losing heat, having to move and not being able to find another place to live, had felt as near to rock bottom as they'd ever been.

"Okay," she said. "We'll stay."

"Yay!" Rachel cheered. "I love it here, Mama. And I love Chloe, and I think she loves me too."

"Chloe?" Carissa asked, not recognizing the name.

"That's Miss Eliza's dog."

"Oh, right." She remembered the mention of a dog from the night before.

"I think she's sleeping in the sunroom at the moment," Hunter's mom said. "She loves to lie in the sun, and it's nice and warm in there too."

"If we're going to stay," Carissa said. "I'll need to go to my place to get some things. Does the bus run near here?"

"I can take you," Hunter said. "As far as I know, the bus doesn't run close by here."

Carissa frowned. "But I use the bus to get to work."

"I think we can probably work something out to get you there and back."

She hated to be relying on them for so much, but it seemed like she didn't have much choice since she'd already agreed to stay with them. She had to get to work somehow, and if Hunter was her only option, then she'd have to accept his offer...again.

As she listened to Rachel chatter on excitedly about the dog, bacon, and Christmas, Carissa wondered if Hunter regretted coming to their door that day not so long ago. Her mind kept wanting to tell her that they'd crashed into Hunter and his family's lives and that they were only tolerating them.

But that was the part of her mind that still carried hurt from the rejection of her and her unborn baby by Rachel's father. He'd told her that she was an inconvenience and her and her baby's presence in his life were not welcome.

In reality, Carissa could see that she and Rachel had been drawn into the Kings' lives, even though she had protested at times. At any of those times of protest, they could have walked away. But they hadn't. Hunter and Heather had kept coming back, helping her and Rachel in all the ways they'd needed help, and more.

Speaking of Heather. Carissa looked around, not seeing any sign of the woman. She needed to thank her for being there to help Rachel when Carissa couldn't.

"Is Heather here?" Carissa asked.

Hunter exchanged a look with his mom, who then said, "She had to go out for a bit, but she'll be back soon."

"Does she live here?"

Hunter nodded. "Yep. She and Mom live here. Hayden lives with me."

"Will Mr. Hayden come here?" Rachel asked.

"Probably," Hunter said. "Though he does like his familiar surroundings."

"These are familiar surroundings," Eliza interjected. "You lived here for most of your lives. You all still have rooms here."

"I know, Mom," Hunter said. "But Hayden has created a new set of familiar surroundings. He'll be here for Christmas, though. I'll make sure of it."

"I want you all here Christmas Eve to spend the night. I think this will be the first year we'll be able to truly celebrate since your dad passed away." For a moment, Eliza fell silent, blinking rapidly. "But I think this is what he would want."

Hunter reached over and covered his mom's hand. "I think you're right, Mom."

Eliza gave him a quick smile. "It's time to bring back happier Christmases, and I think Rachel is just the person to help us do that."

As Carissa thought back over the Christmases since her parents had died, Rachel had been the only reason she'd celebrated. So if Rachel could help bring joy to this house for Christmas, then Carissa was glad that they could do something for the family who had already done so much for them.

CHAPTER 11

Hunter was in the sunroom with his mom and Chloe when Heather returned laden down with bags. "Well, that was certainly a fun errand for you."

Heather grinned. "Never send me off with a command to shop until I drop because you know I'll do just that." She glanced around. "Where are Carissa and Rachel?"

"They're up in their bedroom. Carissa needed to rest, so Rachel went with her to watch some TV while her mom napped."

Heather set the bags down, then dropped onto the couch next to Hunter. "How is Carissa?"

"Better. Her fever has come down, and her dehydration has been resolved. She's continuing on oral antibiotics now, following the IV meds she was given in the hospital, so I think she's on the mend. I've encouraged her to take Monday and Tuesday off, and I think she will, but it sounds like she plans to work the rest of the week."

"I know you wanted them to stay here until after Christmas, but do you think she will?"

"She's already said she would," their mom said. "Rachel's got a couple of days left of school. But Carissa seems okay with her missing them, so it will be easier if they're here since Essie and I can help watch her."

"That's good."

Hunter had to admit he was surprised at how well it had all gone. He'd expected more protest from Carissa. However, the lack of protest was probably less about her giving in because she wanted to be there and more about being practical and making Christmas special for Rachel. That was fine. He could work with that.

"Do you want to text Hayden and see if he wants to come for dinner?" his mom asked.

They hadn't gone to church that morning because of the situation with Carissa, and they hadn't had their usual Sunday dinner yet either. Essie was in the process of rectifying that even though Hunter had told her that they could make a meal for themselves or order some takeout.

"Sure." Hunter dug out his phone and tapped out a quick message to his brother.

Mom wants to know if you'd like to join us for dinner. Carissa and Rachel are here too.

Hayden: *What's on the menu?*

Is that really what matters the most? I promise it will be delicious. Essie's cooking.

Hayden: *I suppose I could come.*

Excellent. I'll let Mom and Essie know. I'll come grab you in an hour or so.

Hayden sent back a thumbs up.

"He says he'll come," Hunter told his mom. "I'll leave in an hour or so to get him."

"What about Carissa?" his mom asked. "She wanted to go get some things from her place."

He looked over at Heather. "Did you get her and Rachel enough things to last a day or two?"

"Yes, but I wouldn't be surprised if she still wanted some of her things from the apartment. Especially anything important to them. It's not like that building has great security."

"Okay. Well, sis, either George can go get Hayden, or you can take Carissa to the apartment," Hunter said.

"Why don't you go to the apartment with her. You'd be more helpful carrying the stuff she might want to bring than I would be."

"And you can leave Rachel with me," his mom said.

"Sounds like a plan."

Heather opened the bags and began to show the contents to his mom, sorting her purchases into two piles. One for Carissa. One for Rachel.

"Oh, those are really lovely, darling."

"And I got them some Christmas pajamas." She gave Hunter a sly look. "As well as Christmas pajamas for *all* of us."

His mom laughed as she clapped her hands in obvious delight. "I can't *wait* for Christmas morning."

Hunter thought about protesting wearing the pajamas. But seeing how happy the idea made his mom, he kept his mouth shut. Until he and his siblings were in their teens, his mom had insisted they all wear matching pajamas for Christmas morning. It was the one and only time of year the three of them agreed to dress alike. Until they didn't. The year they'd turned fifteen, they'd suddenly become too cool for such things.

His dad had donned the Santa suit on Christmas Eve, and he had happily switched that out for Christmas pajamas on Christmas morning. His mom had always had a pair too.

Though wearing Christmas pajamas wasn't exactly high on Hunter's list of things he wanted to do, he would do it for his mom. And if this was a tradition they resurrected, he could probably handle it. Hayden, on the other hand, was probably going to object loudly.

As the piles of purchases grew, Hunter began to worry that Carissa would also object loudly to what Heather had done. He'd told her to buy enough for them for a few days, but this...this was like a whole new wardrobe for each of them.

"Do you want to help me take these things up to Carissa?" Heather asked him.

Hunter hesitated. He was pretty sure that if he went up there, he'd be torn in what to do. A part of him would want to back Heather in her determination to give everything to the pair. But another part of him knew that Carissa was going to object, and he wanted to support her as well.

Pushing to his feet, Hunter allowed Heather to fill his arms with the bags she'd repacked the stacks into. As they walked the hallway to the stairs leading to the second floor where Carissa and Rachel were, Hunter said, "You know Carissa is probably going to not want to accept this stuff, right?"

"I know, and it's not that I want to force it on her," Heather said. "I just want to help them out."

"As long as Carissa doesn't feel like you're giving her all these things because you think she hasn't been able to do a good enough job of taking care of herself and Rachel."

Heather stopped walking and gave him a stricken look. "Do you think that's what she's going to assume?"

"She's been forced to accept a lot of help recently, and I don't want this to be the thing that pushes her over the edge because I think that might also be what makes her push us out of her life. I can't take the risk when she still needs our help."

Heather seemed to consider his words before nodding. "Okay. Let's take all this stuff to my room, then you can go convince her to accept everything."

Hunter laughed. "Well, I'll certainly try, but I'm not going to make any promises."

Heather began to walk again, and Hunter followed her up the stairs to her room. He left the bags there and continued down the hallway to Carissa and Rachel's room. The door stood halfway open, so Hunter could hear the television. He knocked lightly on the door, hoping he didn't wake Carissa.

Rachel appeared in the opening, a big smile on her face. "Hi, Mr. Hunter."

"Hello, sweetheart. Is your mom sleeping?"

"No. She's watching TV with me."

Knocking again, Hunter raised his voice a bit as he said, "Is it okay for me to come in, Carissa?"

"Yes." The reply was softly spoken, but he still heard it.

He pushed the door open enough to see Carissa curled up on the bed, propped against the pillows. The TV was set up to be seen from both the bed and the small sitting area.

"How are you feeling?"

She gave him a wan smile. "Better than yesterday."

"I think we need to ban comparisons to yesterday as a way of determining how you feel. Are you feeling worse than this morning?"

She hesitated then gave a small nod. "Just tired, and my throat is hurting a bit more."

"When did you last take a pain pill?"

"At the hospital."

"That was awhile ago, so I'll get you some pain meds and something cold for your throat. Do you feel up to going to your apartment?"

Another hesitation. "I do need to go."

"Here's the thing," Hunter began. "When I wasn't sure how you'd be feeling, I sent Heather out to pick up a few things for you and Rachel. The problem with Heather is that if you give her the freedom to shop, she tends to go a bit overboard. Okay, more than just a bit. She came home with a *ton* of stuff for you two. She was so excited about it all that I didn't have the heart to tell her to take it back. So you don't *need* to go to the apartment because there are lots of things here for you both. It's just a matter of whether or not you want to accept what Heather has picked out."

"I can't pay you back for all that," she said with a frown.

"I know, but maybe consider it an early Christmas present from Heather."

"Christmas present?" Rachel asked, perking up at the words. "Is it Christmas already?"

"Not quite," Hunter told her with a smile.

"Oh. Well, that's too bad."

"I suppose it would be okay," Carissa said, though she didn't look convinced.

"Good. That way, we won't have to go out in the cold to the apartment until you're feeling better."

"Okay."

"I'll get Heather, then go get you some pain meds," Hunter said before leaving the room.

Heather's door stood open, so he stepped inside, spotting her over by her bed, sorting through the bags again. She glanced at him as he approached. "So? How did it go?"

"She's accepting the things you've bought them as early Christmas presents."

"Nice! Even so, I've sorted through the stuff again and set aside some they can actually use while they're here. Comfortable clothes for Carissa while she's still trying to get better. Plus all the toiletries they'd need."

Hunter smiled. "I think that's an excellent plan. Might be easier for her to accept, then you can give them the rest at Christmas."

"Help me carry this now," Heather said as she held out a bag that she'd filled with some of what she'd purchased.

Hunter took it and then followed his sister as she led the way with her arms full. He hoped that Carissa wouldn't be too overwhelmed because even though Heather had pared down what she was giving them now, it was still quite a lot.

When they walked back into the room, both Carissa's and Rachel's eyes widened at the sight of what they carried.

Heather began talking almost immediately, working hard to convince Carissa why she'd purchased as much as she had. She dove right into showing them what was in the bags, and Hunter decided to just let the two of them sort it out and retreated to his room.

He had a phone call to make.

With everything going on, he couldn't lose the feeling that he needed to ensure that Carissa's apartment was protected while she lived with them. Given the lack of security in the building, it was possible that people could enter it looking for warmth and/or things to steal.

He called his security company and asked to have a guy sent by the house to pick up the key to Carissa's apartment, which he still had from when he'd locked up before heading to the hospital. He also made arrangements for the guy to stay in her apartment until after Christmas.

Though he knew that he could replace anything that was stolen two or three times over without it even putting a dent in his bank account, Hunter also knew that what was there was important to Carissa and Rachel. And because it was important to them, it was important to him.

Important enough that he would pay to keep it safe.

~*~

Carissa could only stare in shock as Heather unfolded and held up one piece of clothing after another for her and Rachel. Then there was a bunch of toiletries. Brands that she recognized as being way out of her price range. Usually, she purchased whatever was on sale when they needed shampoo and other stuff. Being loyal to a brand name wasn't a luxury that she had.

She stared at the mountain of clothing now piled on the end of the bed, uncertain how to feel. On the one hand, she was so grateful for the generosity of these people who had helped her without hesitation. But it was just *so* much. She felt like she would never be able to repay them for everything they'd done for her and Rachel, and she very much did not want to be in their debt for the rest of her life.

"It's too much," she said when Heather finally took a break for a breath. "Way, way too much."

Heather shifted the mountain over so she could sit down on the end of the bed, leaning back against the sleigh-style footboard. The smile she gave Carissa was full of compassion and warmth. "I know it's a lot, but you need stuff while you're here."

"Yes, but not *that* much stuff. Plus, once Hunter takes me to the apartment, I'll be able to get our things."

"I love to shop, so I realize that I went a little overboard. I just really enjoyed having someone to buy stuff for."

Carissa couldn't deny that some of what she'd bought really appealed to her. Namely the leggings and oversized sweaters. They looked cozy and comfortable, which was definitely what she needed right then.

"I don't want to make you feel like you have to take any of this stuff," Heather said. "So if you really feel strongly about it, I'll take it all back. No harm, no foul."

She didn't think that Heather was trying to lay a guilt trip on her. Like she'd take it back if she *had* to.

"Mom, can I please try on that doggy sweatshirt?"

Carissa shifted her attention from Heather to Rachel. "I suppose so. I'd really like to take a shower, if I could."

"Of course, you can. Let me put the toiletries in there for you, then I'll take Rachel with me while you shower."

"Thank you."

"You're more than welcome." Heather hopped off the bed and gathered up the toiletries and carried them into the bathroom.

Carissa hoped she had the strength to take a shower. She still felt wiped out, but she desperately wanted to wash off her stay in the hospital.

She followed Heather into the bathroom, which was huge. It had both a tub and a large shower that looked like it had a bunch of showerheads. This visit was spoiling her and Rachel. It was going to be hard to go back to their tiny apartment.

She just had to remember that this was temporary and not to get too attached to any part of it. Not the super comfortable bed. Not the large television. Not the bathroom that was so much better than their stained-grout shower that barely spit out a firm stream of warm water.

"Is it okay if I dress Rachel in that sweatshirt?"

"Yes. She'd bug endlessly about it if she had to wait."

Heather grinned. "Just text me when you're done. We'll probably be in the sunroom, so I'll come to show you the way down there."

Hunter had given Carissa her purse earlier, along with her cell phone. "I'll do that."

He'd said he was getting her some pain meds and juice, but he'd disappeared and not returned. Hopefully, by the time she was done her shower, he'd be back.

Moving slowly, she removed the clothes she'd had to put back on to leave the hospital, glad to be rid of them. It took her a couple of minutes to figure out how to use the shower. But when she finally stepped into the warm spray, Carissa couldn't help but sigh in appreciation.

The shampoo and conditioner Heather had purchased smelled divine, as did the soap. By the time Carissa stepped from the shower, she was feeling a bit better mentally now that she'd washed away the past couple of days. She was still worn out, however, and it took her a while to dry her hair then go through the clothes to choose something to wear.

In the end, she settled for a pair of black leggings that were thick and warm, as well as an oh-so-soft sweater. She also tugged on a pair of wool socks that had rubber grips on the bottom of them. It all felt so wonderful, and though her energy was zapped, she could still appreciate just how nice the things were that Heather had bought them.

She picked up her phone from the nightstand and tapped out a quick message to let Heather know she was ready. Soon, the woman appeared in her doorway with a smile.

"Ready to go downstairs?" she asked. "Hunter left some pain meds and a glass of orange juice in the sunroom for you."

Carissa was grateful to hear that as she slowly made her way with Heather down the stairs and then through another hallway to a bright sunroom. She gazed around, taking in the Christmas tree tucked in one corner. With three walls that had large windows, she could see the mountain of snow outside. The room itself was cozy with warmth spilling from a small wood-burning stove in another corner of the room.

"Come in and have a seat," Eliza said with a smile. She sat on an overstuffed loveseat with Rachel beside her, a book in her hands.

"Here are the pills Hunter left you," Heather said, gesturing to a small plate and cup on an end table.

Carissa sank down on the couch and picked up the pills. After popping them into her mouth, she swallowed them with a sip of the orange juice. It still hurt to swallow, but not nearly as bad as it had the day before. She sincerely hoped that her recovery happened as quickly as her downward spiral had.

It still amazed her—in a bad way—at how quickly her health had deteriorated. It had to have been a combination of the infections plus the anxiety and stress she'd been under recently. As far as she could tell, those were the only things that could have made the infection progress so quickly.

Of course, it was possible that her lack of good nutrition had impacted things as well. Unfortunately, none of the contributing factors had changed. She still had to find a place to live, and their budget was going to continue to remain tight for the foreseeable future.

She settled back on the couch, her gaze on the snow outside the sunroom, listening as Rachel chatted with Heather and Eliza. After everything the King family had already seen regarding their situation, she no longer worried about what Rachel might say.

CHAPTER 12

As Rachel and Eliza chatted back and forth, Carissa felt a sudden wave of grief. It had been awhile since she'd felt their loss so strongly, but seeing Rachel interact with Eliza made Carissa miss her mom so much. Rachel had no grandparents left now that Carissa's parents had passed away. Her paternal grandparents had never wanted anything to do with her.

Eliza seemed willing to step into that role, at least in the short term. Carissa doubted that they would be as involved in their lives once the holiday season had passed. After that, Carissa would have to explain to Rachel why the King family had only been in their lives for a short time.

"Mama?"

Carissa looked away from the snow to where Rachel sat with Eliza. "Yes, lovey?"

"Are you feeling better?"

She gave Rachel a reassuring smile. "I do, but my throat still hurts a bit. Are you feeling okay?"

Rachel beamed at her. "I feel great, Mama."

Carissa was glad to hear that, and she hoped it stayed that way.

"Where's Mr. Hunter?" Rachel asked Eliza.

"He went to get Hayden, so he can eat dinner with us."

"I like Mr. Hayden," Rachel announced.

"I didn't realize you'd met Hayden," Eliza said.

"He joined us at the Christmas thing we went to the other night," Heather said. "Apparently, his therapist told him to get out more, and he was seeing her yesterday, so Friday night was his last opportunity to do as she'd requested."

"So he couldn't come to the indoor children's party but went out in the freezing cold?"

Heather shrugged. "Don't ask me to explain it. You can ask him about it when he gets here."

"I'll see what kind of mood he's in," Eliza said with a sigh. "I'm sure he'll get defensive about it if I don't phrase my question just right."

"And he might still get defensive even if you do," Heather muttered.

"Mr. Hayden got hurt in a car accident?" Rachel asked.

Eliza nodded. "Yes, he was badly hurt."

Carissa wondered if Hunter had shared with his family the tragedy they shared.

"My nana and papa were in a car accident too," Rachel said.

Eliza looked over at Carissa. "I'm sorry to hear that."

"Thank you." Carissa wasn't going to give details because she had no idea how Eliza would take the information about her parents' death when it was tied so closely to her own husband's demise.

"I can't believe that the sun is setting already," Heather said, changing the subject rather adeptly and probably on purpose. "Four-thirty, and it's already getting dark."

As she said that, the small Christmas tree in one corner of the room suddenly lit up.

"Whoa," Heather said as she jumped. "I keep forgetting you have those things on timers."

Rachel giggled at Heather's reaction. "Magic lights. Poof!"

"Yeah, they do kind of seem like they're magic, don't they?" Eliza said with a grin.

"Did the other trees come on too?" Rachel asked, looking like she was ready to set off on a Christmas tree hunt.

"Yep. They're all set up that way. Makes it easier than having to go around turning all the lights on."

"That's so cool," Rachel said. "We have to plug our lights in every night."

"That can be fun too," Eliza said. "You can be the magician."

Rachel laughed at that. "I like your lights better."

Carissa did too, and now that she'd accepted that they were going to be staying there through the holidays, she was glad that they were surrounded by so many Christmas decorations. It reminded her of their Christmas celebrations before her parents had passed away. Though they hadn't had a large home like the Kings had, they'd had a ton of decorations. Her mom had covered every available surface with Christmas decorations.

Chloe's head popped up, and her gaze went to the hallway that led to the sunroom. Soon, Hunter appeared, with Hayden walking behind him on his crutches.

"Hey, Mr. Hayden," Rachel called out a greeting.

"Hey there, Rachel."

Her brow furrowed as he limped across the room to sit in an armchair. "Do your legs hurt?"

"They kind of hurt every day."

"That's not good," Rachel said, her frown deepening.

Hunter came over and settled onto the couch with Carissa. "You doing okay?"

She nodded, trying not to be drawn in by the concern in his gaze. "Thank you for the pills and orange juice."

He smiled at her. "You're very welcome. Hopefully, you won't need them too much longer."

As she thought about the days ahead, Carissa realized she still needed to phone her bosses to let them know that she wouldn't be able to work for a couple of days. Considering that she was pretty sure that she'd picked the bug up at work, she didn't think it would be too smart to go back and spread it even further. Not that she felt up to working.

Part of her wished that she could just take the whole week off, but that would be unwise given that she needed money more than ever right then. So she would be smart, rest up for a couple of days and then go back to work, provided she felt better.

"Do you think we could go by my apartment at some point in the next day or two?" Carissa asked.

Hunter frowned. "Did you need something in particular?"

"I need my laptop and my work clothes," she said.

His frown eased a bit, but Carissa got the feeling that he was trying to figure out how to not have to take her there. Unfortunately, he was going to be disappointed if that was his goal. She needed those two things most of all, and there was just no getting around it.

"We can go there tomorrow when I get off work. Would that be okay?"

"Yes. That would be fine. Thank you."

She hated to ask him to do anything more for her, but she had no choice. She couldn't get to her apartment on her own since no buses were running from that neighborhood, and she doubted she could afford a taxi.

With all her heart, Carissa wished that she had a way to repay the Kings for everything they had done for her. She couldn't even buy them Christmas presents because she had no way to get to a store, nor did she have the funds to spare.

Maybe once she was in a new apartment, things would settle down enough that she could try to come up with something to show how much she appreciated all they'd done for her and Rachel. What that would be, she had no clue. Hopefully, in the meantime, something would come to mind.

~*~

Hunter swung by Carissa's apartment early the next afternoon, unwilling for her to find out that he'd had someone keeping an eye on things while she wasn't there. He needed to get the key from the guard and let the guy know he had to make himself scarce for a few hours.

Once he had that sorted out, he returned to the house to pick Carissa up. He knew she wasn't feeling one hundred percent, maybe not even seventy-five percent yet. Still, she was definitely better than she'd been a couple of days earlier. The antibiotics were doing their job, and it seemed like her recovery was headed in the right direction.

"Thank you for bringing me," Carissa said as they pulled away from the house.

"You're more than welcome. I'm happy to do that for you." He turned from the driveway out onto the street. "So your boss was okay with you taking a couple of days off?"

"They didn't really have a choice. I can't serve food when I'm not feeling well. In fact, I'm pretty sure I picked this up from someone at work. My one boss said that they had a couple of others out with the same thing. I just hope that I don't pass this on to the rest of you."

"I think we'll be fine," he assured her. "But since we know that you've been sick, if any of the rest of us start to feel sick, we'll know that we need to get to the doctor before it gets too bad."

"Still, I'd hate for anyone else to come down with something this close to Christmas."

Hunter understood what she was saying, but he also didn't want her to blame herself if someone else in the house got sick. That was just how life was sometimes.

It wasn't too long before they pulled up in front of the apartment building. It never looked any better, no matter how many times he came there. It was a hulking gray square that looked as cold on the outside as it was on the inside. There was no image of warmth being projected by this place which had once been home to numerous people.

Though he wished he could hurry Carissa through the cold air into the building, Hunter figured that she wasn't feeling up to hurrying. As it was, she still had to climb several flights of stairs to get to her apartment.

He just hoped that the security guard hadn't left a bunch of stuff out of place. The man had assured him that he'd ordered plenty of takeout on Hunter's dime, and he'd made sure to put everything in the garbage and take it out.

When they reached the apartment, Carissa took a deep breath and let it out. Hunter read it as relief, but he didn't know if it was because she was back in the apartment or that she'd survived the climb.

"I'll just be a couple of minutes," she said as she moved toward the bedroom. When she returned a few minutes later, she had a duffle bag in one hand.

"Here. Let me take that for you." Hunter held out his hand, and she handed the bag over without question. "Whoa. Did you pick up some gold bars while you were in there?"

"Not exactly. Just my old clunker of a laptop, some clothes, and a few books and things I'd bought Rachel for Christmas."

"Anything else you need?"

"I suppose I should make sure there's nothing that can go bad in the fridge," she said as she moved to the kitchen.

138 · KIMBERLY RAE JORDAN

Hunter was checking his phone while he waited when he heard her say, "Well, that's weird."

"What's wrong?" Hunter said as he walked into the kitchen.

"Uh...there's cans of soda in my fridge. I haven't bought soda in forever."

Hunter wanted to shake the security guard for not clearing up everything he'd brought into the apartment. Now he'd have to come clean with Carissa and hope she didn't get mad at him.

"Actually, I've had someone checking on your apartment while you've been with us to make sure no one broke in."

Carissa frowned at him. "And they left soda in my fridge?"

"I guess so."

"So they've been inside my apartment?"

"Yes, but I trust them explicitly. They work for the security company that I use for our homes and offices."

"Thank you for doing that. I know you probably don't think there's much here worth guarding, so I appreciate that you still sent someone by to keep an eye on things." She glanced around. "I know that it might not seem like a lot of stuff, but it's...you know...our stuff."

Hunter couldn't help but reach out and take her hand, waiting until she looked at him before saying, "I know that everything within these walls is important to you and Rachel, and because of that, it's important to me. So yes, it was worth guarding."

Her eyes blinked rapidly, and Hunter wanted to pull her into his arms so she wouldn't start to cry. "Thank you. I'll never be able to repay you for what you've done for us."

When she looked down at where he held her hand, Hunter expected her to pull away. But instead, her fingers tightened around his, as if she needed to hang on. If that was the case, Hunter would gladly be the person she hung on to. In fact, he wanted that more than he'd ever thought he would.

It was something he'd seen between his parents. When his mom had needed support, his dad had been there for her to hold on to. But it hadn't been just his dad supporting his mom. Hunter clearly remembered when his grandma had passed away suddenly. His dad had been absolutely devastated. They'd never seen him like that before, and it had been scary for him and his siblings.

But his mom had stepped right up. She had been his dad's anchor during that time of tremendous grief. When his dad had finally begun to move past that grief, he'd credited his wife for being the support he had needed.

Right at that moment, Carissa needed an anchor, and Hunter wanted to be that for her, even if for just a short time. However, each time they were together, Hunter found himself drawn to her more and more. Her strength. Her determination. Her willingness to do what she had to for Rachel's sake. He knew that his dad would have admired her the way the rest of the family did.

"I know you're struggling right now," Hunter said softly. "But I want you to know that it's not what is defining you. At least in our eyes. When I...we look at you, we see a mother who loves her daughter. Someone who works hard and does their very best to provide a safe life for their child."

Hunter had thought the words would buoy Carissa up. But instead, her shoulders slumped, though she kept her grip on his hand.

"I feel like I'm failing in providing that safe life for Rachel."

The words were whispered, but Hunter heard them as if they'd been shouted. He knew then that they had to make one more stop before going home.

"I want to show you something," Hunter said. "Do you have anything else you need to do here before we go?"

She let go of his hand, then moved back to the fridge. Hunter couldn't see much in the way of fruit or vegetables that would spoil. Carissa emptied the last inch or so of milk from the jug, then rinsed it before putting it in the bin clearly used for recycling.

"I think that's it," she said.

Hunter lifted the duffle bag strap onto his shoulder, then followed Carissa out of the apartment, pausing for a moment to lock it up. He pocketed the key, planning to give it to the security guy when he swung by the house later.

At the SUV, he opened the passenger door for Carissa, waiting for her to settle in before closing it. Rounding to the driver's side, he put the duffle bag on the back seat then got behind the wheel.

"Where are we going?" Carissa asked as he pulled away from the curb.

"Not too far from here." He didn't want to say anything until they got to their destination.

As if realizing that he wasn't going to say anything more, Carissa didn't press for more information. They drove just a few streets over, but the environment improved enough that the buildings didn't look so run down and unsafe. The area had been revitalized in a way that Hunter hoped that rebuilding Carissa's apartment block would do to its surroundings.

When they reached the building, Hunter pulled to a stop at the curb. He climbed out and went around to open Carissa's door.

Carissa paused as she stepped onto the sidewalk and looked up at the six-story building where Christmas lights decorated many of the balconies. "What is this?"

"If you would like, this could be your new home."

He heard her gasp as she pressed a hand to her chest, looking from the building to him. "What?"

"Let's go inside," Hunter said, resting his hand on her back to guide her to the front door.

When they reached the door, he pulled out the set of keys that Heather had returned to him on Friday after she had worked her magic. Perhaps they'd been hasty in preparing the apartment when Carissa hadn't even seen the place yet, let alone agreed to take it. However, Heather had assured him they could return everything if Carissa said she didn't want it.

He held the outer door for her, and they stepped into a warm foyer where there was a security panel people could use to buzz residents of the building. He used the key to open the inner door and led her to an elevator.

Carissa didn't say a word as they got on the elevator. Hunter pressed the button for the sixth floor, then stepped back as it began its smooth climb to the top floor. When the door slid open, she hesitated long enough that the door began to close again.

Hunter reached out to stop the door, then looked at Carissa. "Trust me. You're still in control. This is just an option, okay?"

Her brow furrowed for a moment before she nodded and stepped out of the elevator. He followed her out then led the way to the door at the end of the hallway. Using the other key on the ring, he opened the door and gestured for Carissa to precede him inside.

As he stepped in behind her, the light scent of spices that he associated with Christmas greeted them. It had to be some sort of air freshener that Heather had used because there was no way his sister had been baking.

"This unit became available a couple of weeks ago," Hunter said. "So we thought we'd see if you'd like it."

"I can't afford this," Carissa said, even though she hadn't ventured beyond the small foyer.

"Let's have a look around first," Hunter suggested.

He was hoping that the fact that it wasn't a spacious three-bedroom apartment might make it easier for her to accept that maybe it was not so far out of her price range. It wasn't that he thought she could actually afford the place, but he was willing to give her a discount in memory of his dad.

Hunter knew that his dad would have wished that someone had helped him and his mom out in that way. It wouldn't be the first time they'd done something like this. In fact, his dad had helped many people out, whether it was with a place to stay or help with a job or schooling. His dad had wanted to give breaks to single moms the way he wished people had given his mom a break.

The apartment was small in comparison to his own apartment or his mom's house. Still, it was bigger than where Carissa and Rachel currently lived. It was just a single bedroom, but the room was big enough to allow for a daybed for Rachel and a double bed for Carissa. Both of which were already present in the room.

He just hoped that Carissa could see her and Rachel living there and would accept the spirit in which it was being given. If need be, they could pay a visit to someone on the second floor who had been a recipient of his dad's generosity, so she would know that it wasn't only her that the King family had helped.

CHAPTER 13

Carissa took a few tentative steps further into the apartment. She was torn about how she felt right then. Part of her wanted to accept it without even looking further at it. The place was perfect. The building was not just secure, but it was also still in the area of Rachel's school and the babysitter. Two things she'd prayed they would not have to change after the move.

But there was a part of her that balked at accepting yet one more thing from the King family. She was pretty sure that she wouldn't be able to afford the rent on this apartment, even if it wasn't super fancy.

At Hunter's prompting, she began to wander through the apartment. It was an open floor plan with the kitchen and small dining area to the left of the entrance and the living room in the middle. There was a sliding door that led to a small balcony that looked out on the front street.

There was already furniture in the dining area and the living room, and from a glance in the cupboards in the kitchen, she could see that they were also filled with dishes, pots, and pans. Everything they would need to live in the apartment.

Hunter was silent as he trailed her down the hallway. She was glad to see that there was only one bedroom because that would mean the rent would be closer to what she could afford.

The bedroom was larger than their current one, and it had a double bed against one wall and a daybed against the other. A chest of drawers sat under a large window. It was a bright and cheery room, and Carissa knew that Rachel would love it.

All of it was perfect. So very perfect.

Carissa stood staring into the bathroom, not really seeing anything as she tried to figure out what to do.

"What are your thoughts?" Hunter asked softly.

"It's so nice." She glanced up at him. "But I don't think I can afford it."

"Let's go sit down," he said with a nod of his head to the hallway that led back to the living room.

"No one lives here?" Though it was fully furnished, she hadn't seen any personal items like photos or knickknacks.

"No." Hunter waited for her to sit down on the couch before he took a seat on the love seat that was kitty-corner to the couch. "The apartment's tenant moved out a couple of weeks ago."

"How much is the rent?"

Hunter hesitated then said, "Can I explain something to you before I tell you that?"

Carissa frowned. "Okay?"

"I think I've mentioned that my dad was raised by a single mother who struggled to make ends meet. She worked hard to provide my dad with a good life, though it was a challenge. When my dad's business expanded and his wealth began to increase, he resolved to take care of his mom. But he also wanted to help people—especially single mothers—who might be struggling to care for their children.

"This was the last building he built before he passed away, and several of the tenants are people he helped. For some, he offered subsidized rent. For others, he offered to help pay for education for themselves or their children. For a couple, he was able to find jobs within our company. He didn't view his actions as charity, but as doing for others what he wished someone would have done for his mom."

Carissa let his words sink in. "So everything you've done for us is in honor of your dad?"

Hunter hesitated. "Some of it, yes." He cleared his throat. "Some of it is because of me."

"What do you mean?"

Hunter stared at her for a moment. "I've really enjoyed the time I've been able to spend with you and Rachel. Christmas has been difficult for me...for us...since my dad passed away. He loved Christmas. It was his absolute favorite time of year. This year, meeting you and Rachel has rekindled a love for the holiday within me. Even my mom has seemed to come to life this year because of you and Rachel."

It seemed odd to Carissa that she and Rachel could have had any sort of impact on the lives of people like the Kings. Especially since all they'd done so far was take, take, and take from them. Carissa had felt like they hadn't given them anything in return. But maybe she'd been wrong.

"Here's the deal with the apartment," Hunter said. "The rent will be the same as what you are paying at your old place, all utilities included. The only extras will be your cable and internet. There's one parking spot with the apartment as well."

Carissa felt the constant knot of tension in her shoulders loosen. Was it really that simple? Could this be their new home?

She glanced around the room, trying to imagine them living there. It took no imagination at all. Even now, she could imagine Rachel spinning around, her arms spread wide, her joyful laughter filling the room. Carissa might even join her.

"You don't have to give me an answer right now," Hunter said. "Feel free to think about it as long as you need to."

"Just so long as I decide before the end of the month?"

Hunter gave her a smile. "Well, that would be preferable. Also, if this might help you, the other older gentleman that is still in your apartment building has been offered a studio apartment in this building as well. He too will be offered the same rent as in the old building."

That news did make Carissa feel better about accepting their generosity yet again. "We were the last two people in the building?"

He nodded. "The others who hadn't been moved out at the beginning of the month have already found places."

"Are you going to build a building like this one in the other place?"

"That's the plan. We'll demolish the old building in the new year, then we'll begin preparing to replace it with one like this."

"I'm sure your dad would be happy that you're carrying on his legacy."

Hunter smiled, though there was an edge of sadness to it. "I'd like to think he would be. It was hard, at first, to think about carrying on this type of thing. It took us a full year after his death before we were able to consider how to do this without him."

"I think he'd be very proud of what you've done," Carissa said, feeling confident that that was true even though she didn't know exactly how they'd done it. She might also not know anything about Hunter's dad, but she could see a reflection of the man he must have been through his remaining family members.

"I sure hope so," Hunter said. "He was such a good man, and he never let his success cloud his memory of where he'd come from. I haven't had those experiences myself, but Dad always made sure that we knew that not everyone was as fortunate as us."

Carissa found herself wishing that she'd had the opportunity to get to know Mr. King. It sounded like he would have been happy to meet her and Rachel.

"You and Rachel have drawn us back to what Dad always wanted us to focus on. Yes, he wanted us to be hardworking and doing our best to grow the company's wealth, but not so that we could just buy more houses and nicer cars. He wanted us to use that wealth to help others."

"Like the Christmas party?" Carissa asked.

"Exactly," Hunter said with a smile. "He loved that party, and he would have been disappointed if we'd let that lapse. I'm not sure I'll ever be able to dress up like Santa the way he did. He had a much more outgoing and jovial personality. But we'll always have the party for children. That's a given."

Though she'd been praying about the situation, Carissa had to admit that she hadn't anticipated this type of answer to her prayers. She'd figured that she might end up with the same type of apartment, in the same or slightly better condition as what they currently had. She'd wanted to be able to stay in the neighborhood, not because she liked it, but because it would be best for Rachel to at least be able to finish out the school year without having to change schools.

Now she had the opportunity to live in a nice apartment in the same neighborhood. It was a wonderful answer to prayer.

"I would like to accept your offer of this apartment," Carissa said, knowing that she didn't need to think about it. There was nothing to think about.

Hunter's smile grew. "I'm so glad to hear that. We can move your things over after Christmas, if that's okay. We'd still love to have you stay with us through Christmas."

"We'd like that too." She knew they had everything they needed at the Kings' home, so rushing to move was unnecessary.

"We can bring Rachel to look at the apartment at some point."

"Oh, she'd love that."

"Excellent," Hunter said with a grin. "In the meantime, let's head back."

Hunter used the key to lock up the apartment, then they headed down in the elevator—a working elevator!—and out to his car. Though Carissa still wasn't feeling one hundred percent better physically, emotionally, she felt better than she had in a very long time. The stress had eased, and she was filled with a hope that she hadn't experienced since before her parents' death.

When they got back to the house, dinner was almost ready, so Carissa went upstairs to get freshened up. Hunter carried the duffle bag up for her, then headed down the hallway to his bedroom.

She wasn't sure why he'd stayed at the house instead of going to the apartment he shared with Hayden, but she had to admit that she enjoyed having him around. As did Rachel, if her enthusiastic interactions with the man were anything to go by.

Back down at the dining table, Carissa noticed that Hayden was there again too. Essie and George joined them at the table, which Carissa appreciated. She would have not liked it if the woman had prepared a meal for them but then had eaten her food in the kitchen.

Essie seemed to be less of a servant and more of a family member, which made Carissa happy. She was glad her throat was feeling better, so she could enjoy the food Essie had prepared. It was certainly better than anything Carissa had ever made.

After dinner, Heather produced a game that was suitable for Rachel to play along with the adults. Hayden declined to play, but he didn't leave. He sat on the couch with his mom, and Chloe sat next to him, her head resting on his knee. With regular movements, he petted her head and scratched her ears.

Heather instructed them on how to play the game, which was good because Hunter and Rachel had never played it, and it had been many, many years since Carissa had. *Candyland* wasn't a challenging game, but it still brought out a competitive streak in Heather and Hunter.

Carissa wondered if Rachel would get upset if she didn't win. But when Heather prevailed, it was Hunter who was more upset than Rachel over losing. Eliza had laughed several times as they'd played, and even Hayden had cracked a smile a time or two.

By the time they finished a second game, which Carissa had won, it was time for Rachel to go to bed. After they said goodnight to everyone, they went up to the room where Carissa gave Rachel a bath and washed her hair. Using the blow dryer that Heather had bought them, Carissa made sure her hair was dry before putting her to bed.

They were still sharing a bed, though this one was bigger than any they'd ever slept in before. As Rachel settled under the covers with her book, Carissa wondered how she would like having her own bed. She wasn't going to say anything to her about it, though, until they went to look at the apartment.

"Are you really feeling better, Mama?" Rachel asked when Carissa joined her in the bed after taking a shower and going through her nighttime routine—such as it was.

Carissa turned off the overhead lights, leaving just the lamp on her side of the bed on. As she slid under the thick comforter, she said, "I'm feeling very much better."

"I'm so glad. You were real sick."

"Yes. I was." Carissa hoped that the memory of that day would fade from Rachel's memory. She wanted the memories of this amazing Christmas to be what Rachel remembered when she thought back to this time in her life.

"Do you like Mr. Hunter?" Rachel asked quietly.

"Sure. He's nice. Just like his mom and Heather and Hayden are."

"Do you think he likes us?"

"I'm sure he..." Carissa could only assume her brain was still tired from her body's fight against infection, and that was why it took her as long as it did to understand the point Rachel was trying to make. "Uh...I'm sure he likes a lot of people."

"Maybe he likes us enough so that we could be his family," Rachel said. "He doesn't have a family yet, so that could be us."

Carissa was too tired to have to deal with that bit of Rachel's logic. "That's not quite how it works, lovey. We need to just be glad that they are our friends."

Rachel sighed dramatically. "I have enough friends already, Mama. I want a dad."

She really should have seen this coming and tried to head it off at the pass. Now Carissa had to figure out how to discourage Rachel from looking at Hunter in that way, even though she had to admit that Rachel had chosen a great guy to want as her dad.

Hunter sat at the breakfast nook with a large cup of coffee in front of him. Essie had come bustling in a few minutes earlier, determined to make a big breakfast for everyone.

Sadly, he wouldn't be able to hang around to indulge himself since he had a busy day at work. He wanted to tie up a few loose ends so he could take off the rest of the week. The weather was supposed to be more moderate in the next few days, and he thought it would be fun to get out in the snow with Rachel. He couldn't do that if he was in the office.

"Morning, angel," Essie said with a smile.

Hunter glanced over to see the little girl wander into the kitchen. She wore a pair of pajamas that had unicorns dressed in Christmas colors all over them. Her hair was mussed, which made him think that perhaps she'd woken up and slipped from the bed without waking her mom.

"Morning, Miss Essie." She came over to the breakfast nook and climbed onto the chair next to Hunter. Giving him a smile, she said, "Morning, Mr. Hunter."

"Good morning, sweetheart. How did you sleep?" He lifted his mug to take a sip as he listened to her talk about a dream she'd had—thankfully not a bad one—and about the book she'd read before she fell asleep.

"Would you like a glass of milk, Rachel?" Essie asked.

Rachel nodded. "Yes. Please."

When Essie brought the milk over, she also brought Hunter a plate with a toasted cinnamon roll on it. She made gloriously large cinnamon buns that she then would cut in half and toast. And if they were really lucky, she'd put some icing on them.

"Thank you, Essie," he said. "You are my favorite."

She gave him a quick hug. "I miss having you all here to cook for. Being able to bake and cook for more people is like Christmas came early."

"Well, your talents are very much appreciated."

"I thought we might make some gingerbread and sugar cookies to decorate."

"Today?" Hunter asked after he finished his first delicious bite of the cinnamon bun.

"I'll make the cookies today, but maybe we can decorate them tomorrow."

"That would be perfect as I hope to be off work for the rest of the week. It will free me up to be able to do some stuff around here."

"Excellent plan," Essie said. "It's been awhile since you last took some time off."

"Can I help with the cookies, Miss Essie?" Rachel asked.

"You sure can. In fact, I think I'll need your help."

Hunter wished that Carissa could have taken off the rest of the week too, but he understood why she couldn't...or wouldn't.

Because of that, he would do what he could to make it easier for her by driving her to and from work each day.

"Maybe we could do it after Carissa gets off work," Hunter suggested. "I think she might like to decorate cookies too."

"Mama likes cookies," Rachel volunteered. "But we don't decorate them much."

"It's been a long time since I decorated cookies. Usually, Essie, my mom, and Heather do the decorating."

"But you're gonna help this time?" Rachel asked, her eyes wide. "You're gonna help me?"

"I think I'll probably need *you* to help *me*."

Rachel nodded vigorously. "I'll help you. Mama says I'm a good helper."

Heather came shuffling into the kitchen, and though she looked perfectly made up, she didn't look like she was entirely awake. Mornings had never been her favorite time of day.

"You heading into the office today?" he asked her as she slumped down at the table.

"Yeah. I thought maybe I'd follow your example and finish up anything pressing and take the rest of the week off. I'll still have to do some work, but I can do it from home."

The office would be shut down between Christmas and New Year's except for emergencies that would be screened by a couple of people from their admin team who had taken their paid week off at a different time. Though they preferred people to take off the week between Christmas and New Year's Day, they did try to be flexible with employees who had been with the company for a long time if they wanted time off at a different time.

"Did you want to ride to the office with me?" he asked. "Or are you taking your own car?"

"Are you staying late?" She took the mug of coffee that Essie brought over to her. "Thank you, Essie."

"You're welcome, darling."

"I'm not planning to work late," Hunter said. He ate the last of his cinnamon bun, then finished his coffee. "But I'm going to be leaving pretty soon."

Before she could reply, Carissa showed up wearing an oversized sweatshirt over a pair of leggings. "Morning."

"Coffee, darling?" Essie asked. "Or would juice work better for you this morning?"

Carissa took a moment to answer, perhaps taking stock of how she felt. "I think maybe juice. Thank you."

"We have apple, orange, and cranberry."

"Oh. Cranberry, please."

"Coming right up."

"Did you want breakfast, Heather?" Essie asked.

"I'm not hungry yet," she said with a sigh. "I'll grab something at the office."

"Make sure you do."

"You don't like breakfast?" Rachel asked.

"I like breakfast," Heather assured her. "But usually not this early in the day."

"Well, if you're not eating breakfast, let's go," Hunter said.

He wished they could stay home, but the sooner they got to work, the sooner they could come home.

CHAPTER 14

"Are we picking Hayden up on the way home?" Heather asked as she settled back in her seat with a sigh.

"No," Hunter said as he drove his car up the ramp from the basement garage of the office building. "It doesn't sound like he's had a good day."

"Probably better he doesn't come then."

Hunter knew Heather was right, but he still wished that Hayden could have been there with them. But when his legs were paining him, he was a grump to be around. His temper flared too easily when he was struggling with pain.

The endless round of surgeries and recoveries that he'd need to put his broken body back together still wasn't over. Nor was the battle with his pain. During the first couple of years after the accident, Hayden's injuries had caused him to develop an addiction to pain meds. The fight to get him off them had seemed like adding insult to injury. So now he was left with less effective meds, which meant he had more bad pain days.

"Mom will be disappointed," Heather added. "But she'll understand."

Following their premature birth, Hayden had had to stay in the hospital the longest. Because of that, his mom had already tended to baby him, and since the accident and his brush with death, that had gotten even worse.

"As long as he's with us for Christmas Eve and Christmas Day, I think she'll be okay."

"Do you have all the gifts for Carissa and Rachel?"

"I sure do," Heather said with a laugh. "The IT guys were a big help in getting the laptop for Carissa and the tablet for Rachel, but I have a feeling she's going to protest those."

"I'm just glad she agreed to take the apartment."

"I still think you should have tried to get them into a better neighborhood."

"That would have almost guaranteed she wouldn't take it," Hunter said. "She wants to be able to keep Rachel in her school and still be close to the babysitter."

Heather sighed. "I get that, but I worry about their safety."

Hunter couldn't deny that was also a concern for him, but he couldn't just take over their lives and force them to do what he wanted. And if she'd managed to live safely in a building with basically no security, the new place would be fine.

When they got home, Rachel and Chloe came running to greet them. Well, Rachel came running while Chloe followed at a more sedate pace, as was befitting a dog of her age.

"Hey, Mr. Hunter!" Rachel called out, then lifted her hand.

Hunter gave her a high five then swung her up in his arms. "Where's your mom?"

"In the sunroom with Grandma."

Hunter looked over at Heather and lifted his brows. She just shrugged.

"Grandma?" Hunter asked.

"Yep. She said that I should call her Grandma since I don't have a grandma anymore."

Hunter hoped that Carissa was okay with that. He didn't want her to feel like his mom was trying to force a relationship. Hunter had to admit, though, that he liked the idea of Carissa and Rachel accepting his mom in a role that would hopefully keep them in their lives after Christmas.

Heather headed upstairs while Hunter went to the sunroom with Rachel. Carissa was seated on the couch while his mom was in her usual seat with some yarn and her knitting needles.

"Hello, darling," she said with a smile. "How was your day?"

Setting Rachel on her feet, Hunter went to kiss his mom's cheek. "It was good. Busy, but I got enough done that I can just work from home the rest of the week."

"That's great." She glanced at the door. "Where are Heather and Hayden?"

"Heather went upstairs. Hayden's not having a great day, so he's staying at the apartment."

His mom frowned, but all she said was, "I'll give him a call later."

"So, what did you two do today?" Hunter asked Carissa as he sat down on the couch next to her, glad to see that she looked almost back to normal. With a few days of antibiotics under her belt, she looked to be well on the mend. "Anything fun?"

"We played some games and read some books," Carissa said with a smile. "Essie also had Rachel help make some cookie dough."

Hunter treasured her smiles since they'd been sparingly doled out initially. But even though she was smiling more readily now, he wondered what he could do to give her even more reasons to smile. It seemed only right to want to make her smile more since she'd definitely brought smiles to his face since they'd met.

"Sounds like more fun than I had," Hunter said as Rachel hopped up onto the couch between him and Carissa. "What books were you reading?"

Rachel took the stack Carissa had on her lap and handed them to him. "All of my favorites."

"Are all books your favorite?" Hunter asked, smiling at Carissa over Rachel's head.

"Yep. All books are my favorite," she agreed.

"Do you read them more than once?"

"Oh, she definitely reads them more than once," Carissa said. "And she likes to read them to me more than once too. Several more times than once."

His mom chuckled at that. "I remember that all three of you had a favorite book that you wanted us to read over and over. There were times I wished that you had the same favorite book. But nope, that was never going to happen."

"What was your favorite book, Mr. Hunter?"

"I'm not sure because that was a long time ago."

"Hunter liked books with cars. Hayden's favorites were ones with animals. Heather liked doll books."

"I like animal and doll ones," Rachel said, then looked up at Hunter with a frown. "But I don't really like car ones."

"That's okay. I don't read a lot of books with cars in them anymore."

After a bit more book talk, Hunter excused himself to go upstairs and change out of his business clothes. He was looking forward to not having to wear a suit for awhile.

When he came back downstairs, it was time to eat dinner, so they sat down at the table in the breakfast nook. Though there was a formal dining room, they'd gotten out of the habit of using it. They would eat Christmas dinner there, of course, but all other meals would be at the smaller table.

The meal was lively, and Hunter was glad that Carissa had agreed to stay at the house with Rachel. The pair of them were bringing joy and happiness to a home that had been sad and subdued in recent years. And they were bringing joy and happiness to his heart as well.

And there was more in his heart...but he wasn't sure that Carissa would be open to hear how his feelings for her were growing. But hopefully...maybe...soon.

~*~

Carissa quietly slipped from the bed, then went into the bathroom to change into her work clothes that she'd laid out there the night before. Since Rachel didn't have to go to school, she'd been staying up later than usual, so Carissa didn't want to wake her too early.

She'd explained to Rachel that she'd probably be at work by the time she woke up. Everyone had assured Carissa that they'd make sure that Rachel was okay, which put her mind at ease.

Once she was dressed and ready, she grabbed her pill bottle and quietly made her way out of the room and downstairs to the kitchen. Since it was still so early, even Essie wasn't around yet.

She got a glass of water and took one of her pills, then put the bottle into her purse because she'd have to take another while she was at the restaurant. She'd just put the glass into the dishwasher when she heard movement.

Straightening, she spotted Hunter coming into the kitchen. He was dressed in a pair of black jeans and a dark green turtleneck sweater. She was used to seeing his hair perfectly styled, but right then, it had a softer look to it, like it had no product in it.

"Good morning," he said with a smile that brought to life a swarm of butterflies in her stomach.

"Morning." She felt bad that he'd had to get up before the sun when he wasn't going into work himself, but he'd insisted that it wasn't a problem. Unfortunately, she'd had no choice but to accept his help since no bus ran in that neighborhood, and her car was still doing a bang-up job resembling a boulder in the parking lot at their old apartment block.

"Ready to go?" he asked.

She nodded. "I'm sorry you had to get up so early."

"You don't need to apologize," he said. "I don't mind doing this. In fact, I'm happy to do it for you."

"Thank you."

"If you want to get your boots and jacket, we can go through the back into the garage."

Carissa nodded and went to the large closet in the foyer where she'd hung up the jacket that Heather had purchased for her. After putting on the jacket, she carried her boots to the door where Hunter waited, now wearing a thick jacket and boots.

After she was ready, Hunter led her into the garage to where his SUV was parked. The garage must have been heated because there was no significant shift in temperature from the house to the garage.

Hunter opened the passenger side door for her, waiting until she was settled to close the door. After he slid behind the wheel, he pushed a button on a remote clipped to his visor that made the garage door begin to slide open.

Not long after he'd started the engine, heat began to pour from the vents. Carissa also discovered that the seats must have been heated. Though she hadn't been one to long for wealth—she would have just been happy with enough money to provide a safe environment for Rachel—she had to admit that the luxury of instant heat and warmed seats in a vehicle was very nice.

"Are you sure you feel well enough for work?" Hunter asked as he drove the SUV out of the garage.

"Yes. I'm feeling so much better."

The city was still dark, but that wouldn't have been any different if it had been two hours later since the days were so short this close to Christmas. Streetlights flashed by as Hunter drove, and Christmas music flowed from the speakers. Carissa leaned back in her seat, enjoying the Christmas lights that adorned many houses and buildings along the way.

There wasn't much traffic, so they made good time getting to the restaurant. Hunter's vehicle looked out of place in the somewhat run-down neighborhood, but he didn't seem concerned.

"What time are you done?" he asked after he came to a stop in the small parking lot next to the restaurant.

"I'm off at three-thirty," she said. Carissa wanted to insist that she could make it back on her own, but she didn't bother since she knew he'd just brush the suggestion aside.

"Sounds good. I'll be here."

She undid her seatbelt. "Thank you for the ride."

With a streetlight casting some light into the SUV, Carissa saw Hunter's smile as he said, "You're welcome. I hope you have a good day."

"Thanks. You, too." She opened her door and slid out, then made her way to the back door of the restaurant, bracing herself for a busy day.

The day did indeed end up being as busy as she'd thought it would be. The good thing was that a lot of her regulars had missed her, and when they heard that she'd been sick, they'd tipped better than normal. She appreciated their generosity and wished that she could use some of the tips to buy gifts for the King family. Unfortunately, she had no idea what to get any of them.

When she stepped out the back door just after three-thirty, Hunter was already there waiting for her. He got out and came around to open the door for her, and she let out a long sigh after he shut the door, blocking out the cold air.

She was exhausted after being on her feet all day. More exhausted than she usually would be, making her wonder if perhaps she hadn't been ready to come back to work. But she'd survived, and as long as she had an early night, she'd be okay the next day. She just had to make it through to the end of the week, then she'd be off for a few days.

"Work go okay?" Hunter asked.

She tilted her head toward him and smiled. "Yeah. It was good. Busy, but good."

"Is it just busy because of Christmas?"

"Mainly. Businesses in the area were bringing their employees in for a meal. But the restaurant has good food, so it's always fairly busy." She watched him as he merged with traffic on the street in front of the restaurant. "How was Rachel?"

Hunter gave her a quick smile. "She was just fine. I think she wants to decorate some cookies tonight, so I hope you're ready for that."

She really wasn't, but it wouldn't be the first time she pushed through exhaustion for Rachel's sake.

Carissa sank back in the seat, appreciating the warmth of the car as Hunter drove them home...back to the house. Why she was thinking of it as home, she didn't know. It wasn't home and would never be their home, though the King family had done a superb job of making them feel like it was.

"Are you feeling okay?" Hunter asked. "It wasn't too much today?"

She glanced at him, debating how honest she should be. "I'm a bit tired, but I feel alright."

"I suppose you were on your feet most of your shift?"

"Yeah. The joys of working a service job." It usually wasn't something that bothered her. She'd been working in a service-oriented job for a long time now, and she was quite used to it.

But she'd been worn down both physically and emotionally, making her vulnerable to the infection that struck her down. Hopefully it wouldn't take her long to get back to full health. Especially now that the stress over their living situation had been resolved. And there was no denying that knowing Christmas was going to be incredible for Rachel helped too.

"If you need to take a nap when we get home, feel free to do that. We'll keep Rachel entertained."

She didn't want to take him up on that, but she also didn't want to chance a relapse. "I'll see how I feel. Maybe just an hour or so would be enough."

"Whatever you need," Hunter said.

When they got home, Rachel ran to greet her, wrapping her arms tightly around Carissa's waist. "Mama! I had so much fun!"

Carissa cupped her face in her hands and bent to press a kiss to her forehead. "I'm so glad to hear that, lovey."

As Carissa took off her jacket and boots, Rachel chattered on about everything she'd done that day. Reading books. Coloring pictures. Playing games. Making cookies. She'd definitely been a busy little girl.

"I'm going to take a quick nap," Carissa told her. "Do you want to come with me?"

Rachel frowned. "I don't want to nap, though, Mama."

"That's okay. You don't have to. Just be good, okay?"

"I will," Rachel assured her with an earnest look on her face. "I was good this morning."

"I'm glad to hear that. I love you."

"Love you too, Mama."

Carissa watched as Rachel skipped out of the kitchen and toward the sunroom. She felt a bit guilty about relying on others to watch Rachel after they'd taken care of her all day. But if she was going to last the rest of the day, she needed to get a little rest.

"Go get some rest," Hunter said as his hand gently touched her back. "She'll be fine."

Carissa nodded. "Thank you."

"You're welcome."

Up in their room, Carissa changed out of her work clothes into leggings and a sweatshirt. She set the alarm on her phone for an hour, then crawled under the wonderfully warm and soft comforter on the bed. She let out a long sigh and relaxed into sleep surprisingly quickly.

When her alarm went, Carissa turned it off but was slow to actually crawl out of bed. Finally, she flung back the comforter and sat up, sliding her legs off the bed. She sat for a moment, trying to push back the feeling that all she wanted to do was to sleep for hours more.

She rubbed her hands over her face, then got to her feet and headed to the bathroom. After splashing some water on her face, she fixed her hair. Thankfully, she started to feel a bit more alert and rested, like her body realized it had to be thankful for the hour of sleep she'd gotten.

She wandered downstairs and headed for the sunroom, assuming that would be where she'd find Rachel and whoever was watching her. Sure enough, Rachel was there with Hunter and Eliza. The older woman was knitting while Hunter sat on the floor at the coffee table with Rachel on the other side and the *Candyland* gameboard between them. Carissa wondered how many times they'd played the game that day.

"Hello, darling," Eliza said with a smile. "How was your day?"

Carissa sank down on the couch behind where Rachel was kneeling at the coffee table. "It was good."

"Have you worked there long?" Eliza asked, lowering her wool and needles to her lap.

"For a few years now. I'm thankful for it as they've been good about working with me on my schedule. I usually only work

Monday to Friday, and they let me keep the seven to three-thirty shift. It works best with the babysitter to drop Rachel there in the morning, then she takes her to school with her kids. She also picks Rachel up and keeps her after school until I can get there. And if Rachel is ever sick, my employers have been good about allowing me time off."

"I'm so glad to hear that. It's hard enough to be a single mom, and if you don't have an understanding employer, it's even harder. My Greg used to tell me how hard it was for his mom. That was why he always insisted that if parents needed time off for their children, they be given it."

Her description of her husband fit in with what Hunter had told Carissa about his father. As Carissa's gaze moved to the man who was busy making Rachel laugh, she knew that with an example like he'd had, Hunter would make a good father someday. She wished that Rachel's father had been even half as interested in Rachel as Hunter was.

Carissa still wasn't sure why Hunter was so willing to spend time with Rachel, but she was grateful. He was definitely a man to be admired, and for a moment, she wished that she was the sort of woman that might draw Hunter's attention.

But she knew she wasn't. Hunter needed someone like Heather. Refined. Elegant. Smart. Outgoing. Carissa was the opposite of most of those. The only thing she did have out of that list was her smarts. She'd never really struggled with school, and if things had gone as planned, she would have had her nursing degree by now.

Instead, she was trapped in a low-paying job while she tried to provide for her daughter as best she could. Maybe someday in the future, she'd be able to continue her schooling, but it wasn't going to be right then.

CHAPTER 15

Hunter didn't even bother trying not to laugh at the spectacle in front of him. His mom and sister both had frosting and edible glitter smudges on their faces. They had been so focused on decorating the cookies that they apparently hadn't paid much attention to what was on their hands.

While his mom wasn't the most competitive among them, she could rival them given the right circumstances. Which, apparently, applied in the case of cookie decorating.

As he tackled a few cookies himself, Hunter hadn't felt the need to produce the prettiest ones. He was more about how a cookie tasted than how it looked, though he'd made sure to praise Rachel for how lovely her cookies were decorated.

The little girl also had icing and glitter on her face and in her hair. Carissa, for some reason, had managed to avoid the mess. Probably because she was working much more slowly. Hunter wasn't sure if that was just how she preferred to work or if she was still feeling tired from her full day at work.

Still, he loved the smiles and praise she heaped on Rachel and even spread to his mom and Heather. She'd come so far from the wary woman that he'd met just a few weeks ago. It warmed his heart to think that he might have a played even a small role in giving her a safe space to relax and just enjoy the Christmas season.

He lifted his phone and snapped a few pictures of his mom and Heather to send to Hayden. He wished that his brother had been able to join them. But if his absence now meant that he'd be with them for Christmas, he wouldn't push for his presence before then.

After he'd sent the pictures to Hayden, Hunter took a couple pictures of Rachel and Carissa, but those were just for him. He wanted to capture some memories of the joy that having them around had brought back to his family. It wasn't something he had been able to envision happening since his dad's passing.

But here they were, once again enjoying the holiday with smiles and laughter. And not just that, he'd met a woman who captivated him with her strength, perseverance, and love. He suspected that she would expect him to just walk away once they were settled in their new apartment, but he had no intention of doing that.

He wanted a chance to see if there might be something deeper between them. Though she hadn't even hinted that she might feel something for him, Hunter needed to know for certain. He would never try to force her into a relationship because he knew that he might be seen as being in a position of power over her just by his wealth when compared to her financial struggles. Plus, technically, he would still be her landlord, even if he wasn't directly.

"Mr. Hunter." Rachel tugged on his arm, smearing frosting on the sleeve of his T-shirt. "Do you like my cookies?"

Hunter leaned closer to her to peer at the cookies on the waxed paper that Essie had laid down in front of her. The Christmas tree she'd been working on had a thick, uneven layer of green frosting along with an overabundance of sprinkles. His taste buds rebelled at the idea of eating that much sugar, but he'd do it if it would make Rachel smile.

"They are all lovely, sweetheart." He pointed to a star she'd decorated with another thick layer of yellow frosting and a ton of glitter. "I really like your star."

She beamed up at him, but thankfully, she didn't offer it to him to eat. "Mama, what are you decorating?"

"I'm working on a tree," Carissa said as she used a bag to apply her frosting.

Hunter leaned closer to Carissa and watched as she carefully outlined her tree in green. "You've got a different technique than your daughter."

Carissa looked up with a laugh, her eyes sparkling with humor. "I try to give people a less-frosting option."

He winked at her. "My teeth thank you."

"Santa is going to have a real assortment of cookies to choose from," Carissa said.

"I think we should have a competition," Heather said as she leaned over her cookie, using a toothpick to do something.

"What sort of competition?" Hunter asked.

"I think we should each choose one of our cookies to set out for Santa and see which one he eats."

Rachel looked up from her cookies with a frown. "Won't he eat them all?"

"Maybe," Heather said. "But he's eating a lot of cookies that night, so he might just choose one at each house."

Hunter had no idea if Heather was really in competitive mode or if she was setting Rachel up to win by making sure that hers would be the cookie that "Santa" would eat. He was pretty sure it was the latter, given that she was as smitten by Rachel as he was.

"I think he'll eat mine," Rachel announced.

Hunter had to chuckle at the competitive tone of her pronouncement. They were maybe rubbing off a bit on her. Hopefully Carissa wouldn't get too upset with them.

He'd seen that competitive spirit coming out a bit as they'd played a bunch of different games. The good thing was that when Rachel lost, she didn't get upset. Instead, it seemed to fuel her to try even harder. It was a good trait to see in a child. His dad had never just handed them victories—or anything else, for that matter—when they were kids.

He wanted them to learn not just how to lose but how to come back stronger. If they hadn't been forced to learn that at a young age, they may have completely fallen apart when he'd passed away. But they'd known that they had people relying on them, and they'd needed to step up and try harder than they'd ever tried before to tackle the responsibilities their dad had left them.

Carissa stopped decorating before any of the others were done. She sat back in her chair with a mug in her hand, taking small sips from it as she watched Rachel. Essie had brought mugs of spiced tea to the table for the ladies. Rachel had gotten a glass of milk, while Hunter had decided to opt for coffee since if it kept him up a bit later, it wouldn't matter.

"Do you mind if we take Rachel out with us when we run a few errands tomorrow?" Heather asked.

"It should be okay as long as you have a car seat for her." Carissa frowned. "I should have picked mine up from the apartment."

"I have that one already," Hunter reminded her. "I used it when I drove her to the hospital."

"Oh, right." Carissa gave her head a shake as if trying to get her thoughts in order. "In that case, it's fine to take her with you."

"We'll be back by the time you get home," Eliza said. "I just need to pick up a few more things, and I enjoy having Heather along to help me out."

"Hopefully Rachel behaves."

"I'll behave, Mama," Rachel said, looking up from her cookie. "I'm a good girl."

Carissa smiled at her. "You really are."

Hunter could see that Carissa was beginning to tire, so he wasn't surprised when she encouraged Rachel to finish up her cookies. Rachel frowned for a moment, and Hunter half expected her to protest. Instead, she just sighed and focused on the cookie that was in front of her.

"I'll put the cookies away when the icing has dried a bit more," Essie told her.

"You'll make sure they're okay?" Rachel asked. "Because I want Santa to choose my cookie."

"I will make sure of that, angel." Essie rested her hand briefly on Rachel's head. "And I have no doubt that Santa will decide that your cookie is the best one he's ever seen."

Rachel beamed up at Essie before dropping several more sprinkles on her cookie. "Now it's perfect."

Carissa drained the rest of her mug, then got up and began to clean up her and Rachel's decorating spots.

"Just leave that," Essie said. "I know you've had a long day."

Hunter could see that she was torn between helping and going to bed.

"I hate to leave you with this mess."

"We'll help her clean up," Hunter assured Carissa. "Your day starts earlier than everyone else's."

"Except for yours," Carissa pointed out. "Since you're getting up early too."

Hunter shrugged. "I can nap if I need to."

"If you're sure..."

"We're very sure," his mom said. "I pray you have a good sleep."

"I've been sleeping very well here, so I'm sure I will."

At her mom's prompting, Rachel came to each of them to say goodnight, offering a hug and a kiss, then she followed her mom from the room. Silence hung in the room for a few minutes before Hunter asked. "What are you planning to do with Rachel tomorrow?"

His mom looked up from her cookie and smiled. "We thought it might be nice to take Rachel out to buy something for her mom."

"I thought that might be what you were doing. I'm sure Rachel will love that."

"I just hope she doesn't want to buy her mom anything that was on her list to Santa," Heather said with a chuckle. "We've already purchased the laptop, and I'm afraid that *husband* is a bit beyond my control."

Hunter had forgotten that Rachel had asked Santa for a husband for her mom. Though he couldn't deny being interested in Carissa romantically, it was far too soon for any sort of husband discussion. Hopefully Rachel would understand that and wouldn't be too disappointed when only a laptop showed up from her list and not a husband.

"Are you...uh...feeling things for Carissa?" Heather asked.

Was he ready to talk about the feelings that had stirred to life within him after spending time with Carissa?

"For what it's worth," his mom began, her tone gentle, "I think Carissa is amazing, and Rachel is special. Even if you're not interested in her romantically, I hope they'll continue to be a part of our lives."

"I also think she's amazing." Hunter took another sip of his coffee. "The more time I've spent with her, the more I see qualities that I appreciate about her. I just don't want to put her in an awkward position by expressing my interest if she doesn't share those feelings."

"Why wouldn't she?" his mom asked. "You're amazing."

Heather laughed loudly in response to that. "Of course you're going to think that. He's your son."

"I suppose that's true. I mean, I think you're all amazing."

"Thanks, Mom," Hunter said. "We happen to think you're amazing too."

"And we think you're amazing too, Essie," Heather called out.

"Thanks, darling," she called back. "I'm digging this amazing love fest."

Hunter grinned. He loved his family and wished that Hayden could be there with them. But honestly, if he was there, the lighthearted comments probably wouldn't be happening. Hayden's dour attitude tended to be a damper—not that Hunter held that against him. He couldn't even begin to imagine what it must be like to live with constant pain.

So really, if he had to choose between lighthearted banter and having Hayden there? He'd choose to have Hayden with them every time. Maybe he'd try and talk his brother into coming the next day. However, if he wouldn't come, Hunter might have to consider spending time with him at the apartment for a bit. He didn't like the idea of Hayden being on his own too much, though he did have a housekeeper there to prepare meals and clean for him.

He'd stopped by the apartment for an hour that afternoon before going to pick up Carissa. But Hayden had had physio that morning, so he'd been in pain and grumpy.

As he listened to the women discuss their plans for the next day, Hunter wondered what Hayden would think if Hunter told him about his feelings for Carissa. Hayden already felt like life had dealt him a cruel hand—not just because of the injuries he'd suffered in the accident with their dad, but also because he had the vivid memory of his dad's dying breaths.

Would hearing that Hunter was falling in love be like adding insult to injury?

Hunter wished that he could carry some of his brother's burden. Shoulder some of the pain. But he couldn't. All he could do was offer his support and hope that at the end of the day, his brother wouldn't begrudge him his happiness.

Of course it wouldn't matter if Carissa didn't feel anything for him.

~*~

Sleep was slow to release its hold on Carissa the next morning, and she wanted nothing more than to just sleep until she didn't need to sleep anymore. After turning off her alarm, she sat on the edge of the bed and stared blankly at the floor.

Just two more shifts, and then she'd be off for three days. She wasn't sure why she was feeling so draggy and unsettled. She felt almost completely back to normal, thanks to the antibiotics she'd been on. The worry over the apartment was gone. They were going to have a great Christmas. Nothing should have been causing her to feel so unsettled.

With a brief sigh, she quietly got to her feet and headed for the bathroom. She quickly dressed and fixed her hair before gathering up her purse and phone and leaving the bedroom.

When she spotted Hunter in the kitchen, Carissa felt her heart skip a beat. In a flash, the conversation she'd had with Rachel as she'd sat in the bathroom with her while she'd taken a bath the previous night came flooding back.

"Hey there," Hunter said, a warm smile on his face when he saw her. "Did you sleep okay?"

Not really, but she wasn't going to tell him that because then he'd want to know why she hadn't. "Not too bad. How about you?"

"I always sleep well here," Hunter said as he lifted the travel mug he held to take a sip. "I'm not sure why since I have a better bed at my place."

"Is this the home you grew up in?" Carissa asked.

"Basically, yes. We moved here when we were five or six." He gestured to his travel mug. "Did you want some coffee or some breakfast?"

"No thanks. I'll grab something at the restaurant."

Hunter frowned as he looked more closely at her. "Are you feeling okay?"

She smiled, hoping it would reassure him. The last thing she wanted was for him to start worrying about her again. Concerned Hunter was hard to not want to lean on. But that was not his role in her life. Come the new year, she'd be on her own with Rachel again, and Hunter would be able to get back to his normal life.

"I'm fine. The antibiotics really did their job."

She wasn't sure if he bought it, but he didn't push her. The thing was, she *was* fine. Finer than she'd been in a long time.

"Well, as long as you don't relapse," he said. "We can't have that happening so close to Christmas."

"I don't think there is a chance of that," Carissa assured him.

"Good. I'm not sure my heart could handle seeing you that sick again."

Carissa couldn't keep her eyes from widening at his words. "I'm sorry you had to deal with that."

Hunter shook his head. "I'm not. I'm glad that I was able to be there for you and for Rachel. But that doesn't mean that I want you to ever be that sick again."

"If it's any consolation, I don't think I've ever been that sick before."

"I thought you weren't feeling well that night at the Christmas parade. I should have followed up with you right away."

"I wasn't feeling great," Carissa admitted. "But I didn't think it was that bad. I figured that if I just stayed in bed for the weekend, I'd be fine."

"Well, in the future, if you're not feeling well, you need to let me know."

In the future? Carissa hadn't figured on him staying in their lives once they were moved into the new apartment, but had she been wrong with that assumption?

She nodded, then said, "We should probably go."

Hunter glanced at his watch. "Yep. Don't want you to be late."

It didn't take them long to get their jackets and boots on, then they were on their way through the still-dark streets of the city. Carissa had to admit that it was so nice not to have to stand at a bus stop waiting for a bus that wasn't anywhere near as comfortable or as warm as Hunter's SUV.

Not to mention that she loved the scent of Hunter's cologne that hung subtly in the air inside the car. Being surrounded by that scent was almost like being hugged by him.

"Are you going out with your mom and Heather today too?" she asked, wondering if Rachel was going to get to hang with her second favorite person.

Carissa refused to believe that she had been usurped by Hunter as Rachel's number one.

"Nope. I need to go hang out with Hayden for a bit."

"He didn't want to stay at the house with everyone?"

Hunter sighed. "He's in a lot of pain most of the time, and that makes him grumpy. He can usually contain his grumpiness for a short amount of time. But twenty-four hours a day? I think that would be a challenge for him. He'll try his best for Christmas Eve and Christmas Day, but I think expecting more than that is unrealistic."

"I'm sorry to hear that he's in so much pain," Carissa said.

"We had hoped that he'd get better as time went on. But even after so many surgeries, most days, he's still in a lot of pain."

"Does he need more surgeries?" Carissa asked.

"Yes, but he's resistant, not convinced that they'll make any difference." Hunter shrugged. "And since none of us are the ones who have to deal with the pain and possible disappointment, we can't force him to have them."

"I'm sure it's hard to see him suffer like that."

"He used to be so different. A jokester. Always teasing and laughing. Even though Heather was actually the one born last, he's always been the baby. Probably because he spent the most time in the hospital after we were born. So he's never been a big one for responsibilities. It was sometimes exasperating. Often frustrating. But I'd give anything to have him back the way he was. Instead, I'm left with not being able to do anything for him."

Carissa rested her hand on his arm for a moment. "I think you probably do more for him than you realize."

"I hope you're right because I feel like I've had to focus on the company so much in Dad's absence that I haven't been able to focus on him as much. But I think he tolerates me more than Mom and Heather because he knows he can voice his pain and frustration to me in a way he can't with them."

"That's definitely doing something for him then. We all need a place to feel safe when we're at our worst."

"Where is that safe place for you?" Hunter asked, turning the tables on her.

"I haven't really had that since my parents died," she admitted. "Which is why I know that it can be so important."

"Well, I hope you know that I am happy to be that place for you, just like I am for Hayden."

Her mind headed in the direction that her heart had already been moving before Hunter's words. He was such a caring man. She could see it not just in his actions toward her and Rachel but also for his own family. He'd stepped up in his father's absence and had tried to do the best he could for his family and for the employees who worked at their company.

If only she felt like she was a woman worthy of his attention. But from his own words, she knew that their family made a habit of helping those in need, which was precisely what she and Rachel were.

As they pulled into the parking lot at the restaurant, Carissa gathered up her things. "Thanks again for the ride."

"Anytime." He gave her a smile. "You off at the same time?"

"Yep. Three-thirty."

"I'll see you then."

Carissa climbed out of the warmth of the SUV and tried not to shiver as she hurried across the dimly lit parking lot to the back door that led into the restaurant. Once inside, she inhaled the aroma of coffee and baked goods that the baker had prepared for the breakfast crowd.

After putting her purse, jacket, and boots into her locker, Carissa slipped on her sturdy—and ugly—shoes and tied on her apron that held her order pad and pencil, then clocked in. She greeted the people in the kitchen before making her way out to the dining room, where Christmas music was already playing through the speakers, and braced herself for the busy day ahead.

CHAPTER 16

"Hey, Cari."

Carissa looked up from the food she was loading onto a tray to see the hostess coming toward her. "What's up?"

"A customer just asked specifically to be seated in your section."

"Okay." That wasn't terribly unusual. She had some regulars who preferred her to the other servers, but it wasn't often that Denise sought her out to tell her that. She turned her attention back to the tray. "I'll be out in a minute."

"He's a cutie."

"A cutie?" Carissa frowned as she looked at Denise again. "Who are you talking about?"

"Mr. Tall, Dark, and Handsome."

Carissa stared at the woman for a moment. There was only one person who met that description that she knew. Well, two, actually, but there was no reason why Hayden would be in the restaurant. Of course, there was no reason why Hunter should be there either.

"Okay, thanks." She picked up the tray.

"Is he your boyfriend?"

"I don't have a boyfriend," Carissa murmured as she left the kitchen and made her way through the swinging doors to the dining room.

She didn't look around as she carried the tray to the table she was currently serving. It took her no time at all to place the plates of food onto the table, then refresh their coffees. "Is there anything else I can get for you?"

"We're good," the older woman said. "Thank you."

"Enjoy." Carissa gave them a smile as she turned away from their table to look around the room.

She spotted Hunter right away, and even though he was dressed casually in a pair of jeans and a dark green, long-sleeve shirt, he still looked out of place against the worn décor of the restaurant. He watched her as she made her way toward him and smiled when she reached his table.

"So what brings you by?" she asked, tucking her tray under her arm.

"I've heard good things about the food here, so thought I'd come by a little early and check it out."

"Good choice." She motioned to the menu that laid on the table in front of him. "Have you decided what you'd like?"

"How about you surprise me?"

She lifted her brows. "Uh...well, have you had lunch already?"

"Nope. I decided I'd eat lunch here."

"Anything you absolutely despise?"

"Not really, no."

Leaning closer, she lowered her voice and said, "We don't serve fancy food here."

Hunter smiled. "I'm counting on that."

"Okay. I'll be back in a few. Do you want coffee or something else to drink?"

"Coffee and water would be nice."

She picked up the menu then went to the kitchen to place the order that she hoped Hunter would enjoy. It probably was a copout to order him a burger and fries. But honestly, the burgers at the restaurant were amazing.

With quick movements, she filled a mug with coffee and a glass with water and set them on the tray. After a moment's hesitation, she added a bowl of soup.

Back out at his table, she set the drinks down, then put the stoneware bowl of soup in front of him. "I've ordered you more food, but since it's so cold outside, I thought I'd start you off with a bowl of our tasty beef barley vegetable soup."

Hunter leaned forward and took a sniff. "It smells amazing."

"And it tastes even better, I promise."

He picked up the spoon that rested on the plate under the bowl and ate a spoonful. "Ooh... You are correct."

Carissa couldn't help but smile in response. "Enjoy! I'll be back with the rest of your order in a few minutes."

"Thank you."

She made a tour of her tables, feeling ridiculously pleased that Hunter had shown up to eat a meal where she worked. Best of all, she knew that he was going to love the food. The offerings at the restaurant might not be the fanciest, but Carissa would always maintain that they were the tastiest.

Hunter showing up like he had made him even more attractive. And even though she knew that was the last thing she needed, it warmed her that he'd cared enough about her to make an effort to check out where she worked.

Hunter slid behind the wheel of the SUV, glancing over to make sure that Carissa was buckled in. She had a paper bag in her lap that held a container of the soup as well as a burger and fries. Basically, it was the same order as she'd brought him with the addition of a chocolate milkshake.

Though he'd already been to see Hayden, they were going back to the apartment to drop off the food for him. Hayden had been in a fair amount of pain when Hunter had stopped by earlier, and it was likely he'd tell the housekeeper to not bother making him anything for dinner.

"I kind of thought you might have been overselling the food at your restaurant, but you absolutely weren't," Hunter said as he merged into the afternoon traffic.

Carissa laughed. "Nope. The food has been amazing for as long as I've worked there. And considering the restaurant has been there forever, I would imagine it's been good for a very long time."

"I've eaten at some of the top-rated restaurants, not just in this city but around the world, and they've been good. But honestly, I kind of prefer the tasty, filling food like you served me."

"Our breakfasts are also great."

"Maybe I should hang around for a bit tomorrow to try them out." He almost wished he'd done that for each of the days he'd dropped her off.

It had been interesting to see Carissa at work. It was clear from how she interacted with the customers that she was good at her job. And it seemed like some of those customers were regulars from the way they'd chatted for a bit before she took their orders.

For some reason, he'd kind of assumed that she wasn't happy in her job. Especially since she'd originally been going to school to become a nurse. But even though it might not be her ideal job, she still did it with a smile. That spoke well of her character. She was not just doing what she had to to support her daughter, but she was doing it with grace and a smile.

At the apartment block, he pulled into the underground garage and parked in his reserved spot. "Do you want to come up with me?"

Carissa hesitated. "If Hayden's not feeling well, he might not appreciate that."

Hunter wanted to tell her that she was wrong, but the reality was that she was correct. Hayden preferred to see people on his terms. That day, his preference would probably be to not see anyone except for Hunter.

"You're right," Hunter told her. "I'll just run up real quick and drop off the food. I won't be long."

"No need to rush," she said with a smile. "I'm not going anywhere."

Hunter took the bag from her and got out of the car. Thankfully, the garage area was heated, so he didn't have to worry about her getting cold while she waited for him.

The elevator took him on a rapid ascent from the basement to the top penthouse apartment. Where other floors held two apartments, the upper three floors had just one per floor, and the one he shared with Hayden was the very top floor. It was far more space than he and Hayden needed, but the extra space meant that they had been able to set up a whole room devoted to Hayden's therapy.

Once upstairs, he let himself into the apartment. Immediately he heard the sound of the television, so he made his way to the theater room where he knew he'd find Hayden watching one of his favorite movies. These days, when he wasn't in therapy—both physical and mental—he was either watching television or playing video games. It wasn't the life he'd planned for himself, but it seemed to be the one he'd reduced himself to.

When Hunter sat down on the recliner beside him, Hayden paused the movie and frowned at him. "What brings you back again?"

"Food." Hunter held up the bag. "The best-tasting soup and burger you've probably had in forever."

Hayden gave him a skeptical look. "That's a pretty lofty assumption."

"No assumption. I tried it myself and can attest to how great it is. You won't be disappointed."

Hayden still didn't look convinced.

"Did you eat lunch?" Hunter asked.

After the briefest of hesitations, Hayden shook his head and muttered, "Didn't feel like it."

"Perfect. I'm going to warm this up for you."

He had planned to go right back down, but he hoped Carissa would understand if it took him a couple more minutes. With the bag in hand, he left the room and went to the kitchen.

It didn't take him long to warm up the food and put it on a serving tray, knowing that he had a better chance of getting Hayden to eat it if he could stay where he was. Once everything was set, he went back to the theater room. The movie was still paused, and Hayden sat staring blankly at the screen.

Hunter put the tray of food on the floor, set up a TV tray in front of Hayden, and then put the food on it. "I really do think you'll enjoy it. Even got you a milkshake."

Hayden stared at the food for a moment before reaching out to pick up the milkshake. In the bright light from the screen, Hunter could see that Hayden's hand was shaking as he lifted the cup to his mouth and took a sip.

"Did you want to come to Mom's tonight?" Hunter asked. "I can come back and get you later."

Hayden shook his head without hesitation. "No. I'll be fine."

Hunter felt torn between wanting to spend more time with Carissa and Rachel as well as his mom and Heather and being there for Hayden. He felt selfish for wanting to be in a house filled with Christmas cheer while his brother suffered by himself.

"I'm going to call you later, and I want you to show me you ate."

"Yes, Mom," Hayden said as Hunter made his way out of the room.

Back at the car, he found Carissa sitting with her head tilted back against the seat and her eyes closed. When he settled into his seat behind the wheel, she opened her eyes and straightened.

"Everything okay?"

Hunter sighed. "I guess so. He's in pain, though he won't admit to how much. But when he's watching his favorite movies, that usually means he's hurting pretty bad. He hadn't eaten yet today, so I hope that he'll eat everything I brought him."

"Did you need to stay with him?"

"No. I mean, if I were at work this week, I wouldn't be staying with him. So it's not like I would usually be with him at this time of day. I'll probably come back later and check on him again."

"I never really thought about the other people who had been hurt in that accident, but I guess there must have been a lot of them."

"Yes, there were. I saw the dead and injured numbers not long after the accident, but I didn't pursue any further information."

"I don't know about you, but I had a hard time looking past my own grief and the horrible impact the accident had on my life."

Hunter nodded. "I was struggling to juggle my grief with my need to support my mom, Heather, and Hayden, along with stepping into my dad's shoes at the company." He glanced over at her. "I have to say, I was surprised that our paths actually crossed, and then to find out the tragic connection we have, shocked me."

"It is unlikely, that's for sure," Carissa agreed. "But I'm grateful."

"Me too," Hunter said. "Me too."

When he glanced at her again, their gazes met for a moment. Even as he focused back on the road, the warmth of her gaze lingered in his mind. Was it just gratitude? Or was it possible that she felt something more? Something like he did?

It wasn't long before they got home, and Rachel greeted them excitedly. Hunter figured she was probably bursting to tell her mom about what she'd done that day. But he was sure that his mom and Heather had sworn her to secrecy before they'd taken her out to buy some gifts for her mom.

Knowing Carissa, she'd probably used any available funds to buy gifts for Rachel and purchased nothing for herself. He was curious to see what Rachel had decided would make a good gift for her mom. Her letter to Santa had included fairly lofty requests for her mom. A laptop and a husband.

When he'd first read the letter, he hadn't known what to think. But now...now those requests were understandable, especially coming from Rachel. She wanted things that she thought would make her mom's life easier. Carissa might agree about the laptop, but Hunter wasn't sure how she felt about a husband.

It didn't seem that Rachel's father was in the picture to help Carissa in any way, so maybe Rachel wanted a dad for herself as much as a husband for her mom.

With Carissa busy with Rachel, Hunter took himself up to his bedroom to do some work. He checked his email and responded to some messages from his assistant. The only way he felt right taking this time off was if he kept abreast of things from home.

Thankfully, things were slow since many of the projects in the works were on hold for the holidays. The last of the tenants of the old building would all be out in the week after Christmas, and that project would be ready to move forward in the new year.

He had a couple of other properties he was keeping an eye on. Though he had people who could do the wheelings and dealings on those buildings, his dad had always been very hands-on with the real estate projects, so Hunter tried to do the same whenever possible.

Most divisions of the company were left in the capable hands of managers, people who his dad had trusted implicitly. Though the company was diverse in the businesses under its umbrella, the bulk of the King fortune had come from tech start-ups and world-wide real estate investments.

He knew his dad would want him to make the business his own—to do things his own way—but Hunter's admiration for his dad made that difficult. Maybe in a few more years, he'd begin to do things differently. But really, if things worked the way his dad had always done it, he didn't see the sense of changing anything just for the sake of change.

Once he'd made sure that there wasn't anything pressing that needed his attention, Hunter headed back downstairs. He went to the kitchen and got himself a cup of coffee, then made his way to the sunroom, where he was pretty sure everyone else was hanging out.

Sure enough, his mom was there with Heather and Rachel. Even Essie was there, and she and his mom were talking about something to do with the knitting projects they both held.

Rachel came to join him on the loveseat when he sat down. "I bought Mama presents!"

Hunter smiled at her as he leaned a bit closer and whispered, "What did you get her?"

Rachel shook her head. "It's a *secret.*"

He chuckled. "So I have to wait until Christmas morning to see?"

"Yep. Just like Mama."

"Where is your mama?" he asked.

"She went upstairs to change."

Rachel had barely said that when Carissa appeared. She looked warm and comfortable in a pair of sweats and a sweater.

He had thought she might take a nap, but she didn't appear to be as tired as she had been the day before.

Hunter knew that she still had a few days of antibiotics to take yet, but it seemed that perhaps she was well and truly recovered from the infection that had hit her so hard. He was relieved to see her healthy and, if he wasn't wrong, happy.

She settled onto the other end of the loveseat with Rachel sandwiched between them. The little girl had pulled her knees up and had a book propped on them, apparently happy to ignore the adult conversation while she read.

Contentment filled Hunter, though he still wished that Hayden could be there with them. However, it was Hayden's choice to stay away. Hunter had to accept that and not let his brother's absence keep him from enjoying this time with the woman he was falling in love with and her adorable daughter.

CHAPTER 17

Even though she wasn't working that day and hadn't set her alarm, Carissa was still awake early. But instead of getting out of bed right away, she curled on her side under the covers, enjoying the quiet comfort of a slow start to the morning.

Once Rachel woke up, the quiet would be gone as the excitement for the day grew. Though she'd initially thought that the King family were doing her a favor by giving her and Rachel a wonderful Christmas, she'd come to understand that having Rachel there was something that brought them joy as well.

Carissa was well aware that Christmas seemed to take on a new level of excitement when a child was involved. And if having Rachel around helped do that for the Kings, Carissa was happy they could be there for them.

The only thing she worried about was how she and Rachel would feel once they were back on their own. Over the past four years, she'd tried not to dwell on how alone she and Rachel were.

Only four when her grandparents had died, Rachel had been aware of their absence in their lives, but she'd seemed to adapt fairly quickly. It was Carissa who had remembered how much her parents' love and support had impacted their lives and how alone she and Rachel really were without it.

As the months...then years...had passed, they'd settled into life with just the two of them. But now, Rachel had had a taste of what it would be like to have more people in her life. More people who clearly adored her. When they went back to their solitary life, Rachel was going to miss these people.

And though Carissa might want to deny that she'd miss them too, she knew that she would. Especially Hunter, who had been a steadying influence in their lives almost from the moment she'd seen him through the opening in the apartment door.

How things had changed in the weeks since that day.

"Is it Christmas, Mama?"

Carissa smiled at Rachel's sleepy words. "Not just yet. It's Christmas Eve."

"Santa comes tonight?" she asked.

"Yep." Carissa hadn't been so sure that Santa would come through when it was just the two of them, but she had a feeling that the jolly old man was going to be incredibly generous with Rachel this year.

"I've been a good girl, right?"

Carissa reached out and pulled Rachel into her arms, snuggling with her under the covers. She pressed a kiss to her temple. "The very best little girl."

"And you've been the very best mama."

"I love you."

"Love you too, Mama."

She knew that the cuddles wouldn't last long that day, which made her a little sad. They usually spent a good portion of their mornings on the weekends cuddling in bed because it was the warmest place in their apartment. But warmth wasn't a consideration in the large house that was expertly heated.

Sure enough, it wasn't long before Rachel began to wiggle and squirm. Finally, Carissa caved and got out of bed with her. A glance at the alarm clock showed that it was just after eight.

She helped her change into a pair of soft sweatpants and a long-sleeve T-shirt with a unicorn on the front of it. After she'd fixed Rachel's hair, Carissa changed into a pair of thick leggings and an oversized red sweater, then fixed her own hair and applied a small amount of makeup.

At some point that day, she needed to corral Rachel long enough to make some cards for the Kings. On her lunch break the previous day, she'd gone to a nearby store and picked up some card stock, crayons, and markers. She had resigned herself to not having gifts for the Kings, but she did want to give them something from Rachel. And since Rachel's creative skill was currently limited to coloring, pictures or cards were what she could give them.

By the time Carissa was ready to make an appearance, Rachel was dancing on her toes near the door. "C'mon, Mama. Let's go."

"Alright, lovey. But you need to be quiet until we get downstairs because others might still be sleeping."

Rachel held a finger to her lips and nodded.

Hand in hand, they left the room and quietly made their way downstairs. The aroma of coffee hung in the air, and Carissa looked forward to her first cup of the day.

When they walked into the kitchen, she spotted Essie at the island counter while Hunter sat on a stool across from her. He had his elbows propped on the counter with a mug of coffee cupped between his hands.

Smiling, he said, "Good morning, you lovely ladies."

"Morning, Mr. Hunter!" Rachel let go of Carissa's hand and skipped over to where Hunter sat. She climbed up on the stool next to him and leaned her head against his shoulder for a moment.

When Hunter's expression softened with affection, Carissa had to swallow against the swell of emotion within her. This man could have helped them without ever interacting with her daughter. But rather than ignoring Rachel, he'd spoken with her.

Carissa was pretty sure that he'd used Rachel to get her to agree to things, but she really couldn't find it in her heart to be mad about that. Especially because, for the first time since falling for Rachel's father so many years ago, her heart was once again on the line.

She didn't think there was much chance of him returning her feelings, but hopefully, he would consider them friends so that he'd still be around. For Rachel's sake.

~*~

Hunter savored the sips of strong black coffee that Essie had made for him when he'd wandered into the kitchen a little while ago, listening as Rachel chattered on about Santa coming later that night.

His gaze followed Carissa as she poured herself a cup of coffee then doctored it with flavored creamer. She stood on the other side of the island, hip leaned against it as she took her first sip of coffee.

"Is there anything I can do to help you, Essie?" she asked.

Essie smiled at her before going back to the pancake batter she was mixing. "I think I'm okay at the moment."

"Essie is your ultimate organizer," Hunter told her. "She figures everything down to the minute and rarely, if ever, lets any of us help her."

He could see that it didn't sit well with Carissa that Essie did everything when it came to cooking their meals. Though he wished he could help her understand, he knew that Carissa would need to hear from Essie how she felt about her role within the King family.

Almost from the start of her employment, Essie had been one of the family. Watching her and George fall in love and get married had been fun, drawing them all even closer. As far as Hunter was concerned, the pair were like a second set of parents.

The kitchen had become Essie's domain, and they'd stopped trying to help her when she insisted she didn't need it. And given how little they knew about cooking, it was probably less hassle for her to do it herself than to have them underfoot.

"I have perfected the art of cooking for this family, and I truly enjoy it." Essie slipped her arm around Carissa. "Don't ever doubt that I'm exactly where I want to be. What I do here might be my job, but I love doing it so much that it doesn't feel like a job. Not everyone can say that."

Carissa nodded. "I do enjoy what I do, but not enough to say it doesn't feel like a job."

"Well, I'm glad you enjoy what you do. That is important too." She pointed to where Hunter and Rachel sat. "Now go have a seat and just enjoy the next couple of days."

Carissa hesitated only a moment before bringing her cup of coffee around the counter and sitting down on the stool next to Rachel. With Christmas music playing in the background, Hunter felt a swell of contentment he hadn't felt in several years.

He still wished his dad could be there because he knew he would have loved to have Rachel and Carissa with them for the holiday. But even without him there, Hunter was...content. He had a feeling that his mom and Heather probably felt similarly. It was only Hayden who would be struggling.

Hayden had told Hunter that he'd be at the house by mid-afternoon, in time to eat and then attend the Christmas Eve service at their church.

"Do you have plans to attend church this evening?" Hunter asked, realizing he hadn't asked earlier. He'd just assumed that Carissa and Rachel would go with them.

Carissa glanced at him before looking down at her coffee. "No. We haven't been able to attend church since my car bit the dust."

"No bus service?"

"Nope. I was planning to see if I could find a church closer to where we lived but hadn't managed that yet."

"Well, we're planning to attend the Christmas Eve service at our church, so you're more than welcome to come with us. In fact, we'd love it if you would."

"I want to go, Mama," Rachel piped up.

"Sure. That would be lovely. I always enjoy a Christmas Eve service."

"I haven't always recently," he said. "But I'm feeling optimistic this year."

Carissa's brows rose slightly at his words, making him wish that he could read her mind. "That's good. I hope you do enjoy it."

"I really think I will," Hunter said confidently. That might not have been the case had he not met her and Rachel. But since he had, he was looking forward to sharing Christmas with them.

As the aroma of pancakes began to fill the air, Hunter's stomach rumbled in appreciation. Rachel looked up at him and giggled.

"Well, I don't know about you, sweetheart, but I'm starving."

"I'm hungry too," she told him. "And I looooove pancakes."

Hunter glanced up to see an adoring look on Carissa's face as she watched her daughter. Though he'd thought she was beautiful from the first moment they met, he was so glad to see that the tension and worry were absent from her face now.

He wondered how she would react if he asked her out on a date. It had been a few years since his last date, so he felt a bit like he was out of practice. Since his dad's death, he hadn't felt inclined to start a relationship, especially when so much of his attention had been focused on his family and the business.

Now though, he found himself wanting to make the time for something more in his life. But not just for anyone. It was Carissa and Rachel who had captured his attention, and it was encouraging that he didn't have to worry about how his family felt about the pair. There was no doubt that they would support a relationship between him and Carissa.

Or at least he hoped they would.

Before his dad's death, his mom had hounded all three of them to find themselves a spouse and give her grandbabies. After the accident, it seemed as if she realized that relationships were not in the immediate offing, and she'd let the matter drop.

He had turned a corner this year with his grief, and he hoped that Heather would follow soon. Hayden...well, Hunter understood that his road back from the trauma of the accident would be longer, and he'd never likely be able to completely move on from what he had suffered. But he wanted peace and happiness for Hayden in whatever form that might take.

Essie slid plates with pancakes across the island for each of them. "There you go, you starving people."

Rachel pulled her plate closer and took a deep breath. "Yum!"

"What do you say to Essie?" Carissa prompted gently.

"Thank you, Miss Essie!"

"You're welcome, angel," Essie said with an indulgent smile.

Yeah. He wasn't the only one who was smitten by these two. "Yes. Thank you, Essie."

Carissa murmured her thanks as well, then said, "These look delicious."

Hunter could imagine sitting with the two of them, long into the future, enjoying a Christmas Eve breakfast of pancakes. The future didn't look quite as dim as it had just a few months ago.

They may have shared a tragedy in their lives, and maybe the worst of circumstances had brought them together, but Hunter knew that they could move forward in joy and love. The pair of them already had a special place in his heart that no one else had ever held.

His prayer was that Carissa would look beyond the things that would keep them apart and see that as long as their hearts and minds were in sync, none of the rest mattered at all.

CHAPTER 18

Carissa watched the city slip by in the darkness as they made their way to the Kings' church. She, Rachel, and Heather were riding in Hunter's SUV, while Eliza, Hayden, and Essie went in another vehicle with Essie's husband, George.

"Will Santa be there?" Rachel asked.

"No," Heather said. "Not at the church. He'll come by the house after we're all asleep."

"But what about the alarm?"

"What about it?"

"Can he get into the house since you have an alarm?"

Carissa remembered Rachel asking Hunter about the panel at the wall. Clearly none of them had thought about how she'd tie that to Santa needing access to the house.

"Oh. Well, uh, Hunter?"

"Santa doesn't come through the doors," Hunter said. "So he doesn't have to worry about the alarm. He comes through the chimney."

"Can someone else come through the chimney?" Rachel asked, worry in her voice.

Though Carissa didn't want Rachel to be concerned about safety in the Kings' home, she couldn't help but smile as she waited for Hunter to explain away that one too.

"Not everyone can get to the chimney," Hunter explained. "It's high in the air, so Santa uses his reindeer to get up on the roof."

"Oh." Rachel paused then said, "Can I see the reindeer?"

"Not tonight. Santa doesn't come until we go to sleep."

Carissa had to admire how Hunter managed to field each of Rachel's questions and concerns. He seemed to be a natural at it.

"How did Santa get into our apartment, Mama?" Rachel asked from the back seat. "We don't have a chimney."

"My word, she's a smart one," Hunter murmured, making Carissa laugh.

"I don't know," Carissa said. "We were asleep when he came."

"Well, you're keeping the mystery alive."

Carissa couldn't help but smile at Hunter when he glanced at her. "It's easier than trying to keep answering her questions."

Rachel seemed to be satisfied with the answers that had been given to her since she stopped asking about Santa.

It wasn't long before they pulled into the parking lot of a large church. Carissa had expected Hunter to park and then they'd all walk together into the church, but instead, he circled around to the front doors of the church.

"Out we get," Heather said, then opened her door.

Carissa glanced at Hunter before pushing open her door and climbing out. Rachel was standing with Heather, and after Carissa shut her door, Hunter pulled away. The other car pulled up right then, so they waited for Eliza, Essie, and Hayden to join them.

It was a chilly night, so Carissa was glad to walk into the warmth of the church. There were a lot of people wandering around, but since the church was so big, it didn't feel too crowded.

Eliza led them into a nearby coatroom where they all hung up their jackets. By the time they walked out again, Hunter and George were coming toward them. They waited for them to hang up their jackets then they headed toward the sanctuary with Eliza, Essie and George leading the way.

Carissa held Rachel's hand, and she was surprised—and yet maybe not—when she glanced over and saw that Rachel had also taken Hunter's hand. Heather and Hayden followed behind them, and she could only imagine what they must think.

She'd thought they might go right to the front, but Eliza stopped at a pew near the back. She led the way into the pew, leaving Hayden to be the last into the row.

When they settled down on the pew, Rachel perched on the edge of it between Hunter and Carissa. Hunter put his arm on the back of the pew, which meant his hand rested lightly against Carissa's back.

For a moment, she felt like this was where they belonged. That these people were family to them now. But she knew that wasn't the case.

The Kings had been incredibly generous, and Carissa knew she shouldn't want more. All she had to offer them right then was her daughter. The light in her own life had become a light in their lives as well. She had seen that in the days they'd been in the King home.

Carissa kind of felt like she was just along for the ride. That Rachel was the big draw for the Kings. Rachel had only brought them joy and laughter, while Carissa had in many ways, been a burden.

Her hands clenched into fists in her lap, and she tried to push those thoughts from her mind. At least for the next day. Rachel deserved her mother to be present and happy for her while celebrating their favorite holiday.

So while her heart ached a little at the idea of being a burden to people, Carissa forced herself to look around the sanctuary. The stage had three different Christmas trees on it, each with lots of white lights and tasteful red and green decorations.

As she watched, the choir began to file into the pews on the stage that faced the congregation. They wore alternately green and red gowns that just added to the Christmas theme in the sanctuary.

Rachel slid off the pew to stand, gripping the back of the pew in front of them. Thankfully, there was no one directly in front of her, so she could see the stage better when she stood.

Soon, the lights in the sanctuary dimmed, leaving only the ones over the stage on. The choir stood and began to sing *O Come All Ye Faithful.* Rachel swayed in time with the choir, clearly in her element with the music.

Carissa exhaled, determined to enjoy that evening and the next day.

For the next hour, there was more choral singing, some readings, a few special numbers, and even some congregational singing. When they were invited to stand and sing *Joy to the World,* Hunter got to his feet then bent and lifted Rachel up into his arms. Her joy was evident on her face as she rested her arm on his shoulders and began to sing loudly.

Hunter beamed at Rachel, but when he looked over at Carissa, his smile softened, turning more affectionate. Carissa didn't know what to do with that. Didn't know how to interpret a look like that from him.

Instead, she just smiled back at the two of them, then turned her attention to the front of the church. Her confusion and worries over how things might be after they were in their own apartment could wait for another day.

By the time the last song was sung, Carissa had managed to corral her thoughts and emotions. As they stood to exit the sanctuary, Hunter once again picked Rachel up, likely to keep her from getting overrun by the crowd that was more noticeable now that they were all trying to leave the church at the same time.

"Wait here," Hunter said once they'd gotten their coats on. "George and I will get the cars."

It wasn't Carissa's place to object and say that they'd walk out with him, so she stayed close to the others, holding Rachel's hand as they waited.

"It's almost time for Santa to come," Rachel announced as she danced from one foot to another.

"You have to go to sleep first, love," Carissa reminded her.

She wasn't sure how that was going to work since they'd been going to bed at the same time for most of the week. That night, she wanted to have time to wrap the few gifts she had for Rachel and have them ready for the morning.

Part of her was worried that whatever her daughter got from Santa and the Kings would completely overshadow what she'd been able to get for her. But there was nothing she could do about it. She still didn't have the money to buy her anything more.

"They're here," Hayden said from his spot by the door.

Using his cane, he limped out the door with the rest of them following. Once again, she ended up in the front seat beside Hunter while Heather and Rachel got in the back.

There was Christmas music playing on the radio, and as they drove, Carissa realized that it had started to snow while they were in the church. It wasn't a heavy snow, just light flakes, sparkling a bit like diamonds in the night sky. The Christmas lights on the buildings and homes they passed seemed to shine more brightly too.

When they got back to the house, Essie didn't take long to bring out the food she'd spent the day preparing. It wasn't a full-blown meal because she wouldn't have been able to attend church with them if she'd been focused on cooking a meal. Instead, there was a large assortment of appetizers. All of them yummy.

It reminded her a bit of the children's Christmas party and all the appetizers Eliza and Heather had sent home with them. Rachel had loved them, and she loved these ones too, calling them tiny food.

They took their plates of appetizers into the living room. A room they'd not used much of in the time they'd been there. It was beautifully decorated with a large tree in front of the window that had tons of lights on it. There was a fire blazing in the fireplace, giving the large room a cozy feel.

"How did you enjoy the service?" Hunter asked as he sat down beside Carissa on the loveseat. Rachel was kneeling on the floor with her plate of food on the coffee table.

"It was beautiful," she said. "I always love the music at this time of year."

"Well, it was quite clear that Rachel has heard it a lot." He smiled broadly. "She knew the words to a lot of the songs. Especially *Joy to the World.*"

"That's one of her favorites. She says it's because it has her name in the title."

"Joy? I mean, I would assume her name isn't *to* or *the* or *world.*"

Carissa chuckled. "I wouldn't do that to my child. Yes. Her middle name is Joy. Just like mine."

"Rachel Joy and Carissa Joy?"

"Yep."

"That's neat that you share that name."

"Rachel thinks so too."

"Well, she's certainly lived up to her name," Hunter said. "She's brought a lot of joy to our lives."

Carissa's gaze lingered on Rachel as she talked to Heather who was seated on the floor across the coffee table from her. "Mine too."

"She's not the only one though."

Carissa looked away from Rachel to meet Hunter's gaze, his expression once again affectionate as he looked at her. Her breath caught in her lungs, but she was still unwilling to read anything into his expression or his words.

"Mama!" Rachel turned to look up at her, breaking the moment between Carissa and Hunter. "Is it time for bed yet?"

Carissa smiled at Rachel's unusual eagerness to go to bed. Glancing at the clock, she saw it was just eight-thirty, which was around her normal bedtime, but she'd sort of hoped she would stay up a bit later so that she wasn't awake at the crack of dawn the next morning.

"Not quite yet," she told her. "Are you done eating?"

"Maybe I could have another cookie?"

"Sure." Carissa got to her feet and held out her hand. "I think I'd like one too."

They went back into the kitchen where Carissa helped Rachel choose one of the cookies that they'd decorated earlier in the week. There were plenty of other desserts, and since she'd already had a cookie, she picked up a decadent looking brownie that appeared to have chocolate chunks and nuts inside it.

It had been a long time since she'd worried about gaining weight over the holidays, but she could see that it might happen that year. Not that she was concerned about gaining weight. She'd lost weight over the past few years, so if she gained some, that might actually be a good thing.

"Do you want some coffee?" Essie asked as she walked into the kitchen with a couple of plates in her hands.

"I'm not sure I should be drinking caffeine at this time of night," she said, though it was tempting.

"I'll make a pot of decaf. Eliza doesn't want regular coffee either."

Rachel had left to go back to the living room, so Carissa stayed to help Essie prepare the coffee. Hunter wandered in a few minutes later and stood looking over the desserts.

"These all look so wonderful, Essie," Hunter said. "I don't know where to start."

"One of each might be a good place," Essie told him with a laugh.

"I don't think so."

"Well, put an assortment on a plate, and you and Hayden can share them."

Carissa watched as Hunter carefully began to fill a plate with the bite size desserts. He looked up and smiled. "Did you get some dessert?"

"I got a brownie."

"Just one? I think it's against Christmas rules to only eat one piece of dessert."

"I might eat something else. It really is hard to just pick one."

Hunter took a bite of brownie and hummed his appreciation. "At least Essie cuts these small enough that you don't feel too guilty for eating more than one."

Essie set a tray on the counter in front of Carissa. "You can put those mugs on there," she said, pointing to a mug tree that held several mugs with Christmas designs on them.

When the tray held the mugs as well as a cream and sugar set, Hunter said, "Why don't you carry the desserts and I'll take the tray."

"Thank you," Carissa said.

"You are more than welcome." He flashed her a broad smile as he motioned for her to go ahead of him out of the kitchen.

Back in the living room, they set everything on the coffee table, and Essie showed up a couple of minutes later with a coffee carafe.

Hayden sat slumped in an easy chair, but he perked up a bit at the prospect of coffee and dessert. Carissa watched as Hunter poured a cup of coffee then added some cream and sugar to it before handing it to Hayden.

He did it all without making any sort of deal about it, and Carissa was sure that Hayden appreciated that. It showed Hunter's caring nature, and if that wasn't the most attractive thing, Carissa didn't know what was.

But the last thing she needed was something *more* attractive about Hunter. She was sure the man wasn't perfect, but so far, everything she'd seen about him had been positive...and attractive.

She picked up her brownie and took a bite, needing something else to focus on. Yummy, tasty, chocolate perfection. It was absolutely delicious. But Hunter still held more appeal for her.

CHAPTER 19

Just after nine o'clock, Carissa finally gave in to Rachel's request to go to bed, but first, they had something else to do.

"Let's go get a plate ready for Santa," Essie said.

Heather got to her feet. "Remember that we're supposed to put out one cookie that each of us decorated."

Carissa smiled as the two followed Essie into the kitchen, then turned to look at Hunter. "Are you going to be the one eating the cookie tonight?"

He leaned back against the couch, hooking his arm on the back of it. "I'll make the sacrifice and take one for the team."

"Such a hardship," Hayden scoffed. "Eating one of Essie's cookies."

"Well, Rachel's cookies had about an inch of frosting on them, so I might go into sugar shock."

"Are you only eating one?" Hayden asked.

"Well, I figured that I'd take a bite of each of them, but that I'd eat all of Rachel's cookie, so she thinks that Santa liked hers best."

"This glimpse behind the curtain is terribly disheartening," Hayden muttered.

"Oh, we're doing even more," Eliza told him. "Essie has plans to leave carrots for the reindeer. You could eat those if you'd like, Hayden."

"Uh...I think I'd rather eat the cookies."

When they heard Essie and Rachel's voices, conversation stopped. Rachel appeared with a plate clutched in her hands.

"Where should we put it?" she asked.

"How about on the table by the chair next to the chimney," Heather suggested as she followed them in. "That way, Santa can sit down for a few minutes to rest after lugging all the presents inside."

Rachel walked over to the table and set the plate down. Essie put the glass of milk and the carrot she carried next to the plate.

"That's perfect," Rachel declared. "Now I need to go to bed so Santa can come."

"Say goodnight, lovey."

Rachel went around to everyone in the room and gave them each a hug as she said goodnight. When she approached Hayden, Carissa wasn't sure how the man would react. But rather than say anything, he just leaned forward and let Rachel wrap her arms around his neck.

"Goodnight, Mr. Hayden. See you in the morning."

"Goodnight, sweetheart."

"Be sure to wear your Christmas pajamas," Heather reminded her. "We're all going to be wearing them."

Hayden gave a huff of irritation, but Carissa had a feeling that when she saw him in the morning, he'd be wearing Christmas pajamas too.

"Goodnight, Mr. Hunter." Rachel gave him a hug. "Be sure to tell Santa that I love him."

Hunter chuckled. "I will."

Once Rachel had said goodnight to everyone, Carissa said her own goodnight. "I'll probably just stay upstairs with her, so I'll see you all in the morning."

She would have liked to have stayed in the living room, visiting with the others and enjoying the Christmas atmosphere. However, she still had a few things to do once Rachel was asleep, so after they'd said goodnight, they walked hand-in-hand up the stairs to their bedroom.

Before Rachel got ready for bed, Carissa had her spend a little time creating cards for the Kings and Essie and George. Once that was done, Rachel was more than happy to go through her bedtime routine and even told Carissa she didn't need a story. Clear evidence that the girl was determined to fall asleep so that Santa could come.

Carissa kind of thought that Rachel would have a hard time falling asleep. But even though she didn't turn off all the lights, Rachel fell asleep quickly.

After making sure she was really sound asleep, Carissa gathered up the few things she'd bought for Rachel as well as the stuff she'd purchased to wrap the gifts. She settled on the floor and quietly began to wrap everything.

Carissa was well aware that once Rachel got to the gifts that were likely to be under the tree in the living room, she probably would forget all about the small things Carissa had bought for her. Because of that, she decided to keep the gifts in their room for Rachel to open before they went downstairs.

When she was finally done with the wrapping, she took the small stack of gifts and quietly set it on the nightstand on Rachel's side of the bed. In the dim light of the lamp, Carissa stood watching her daughter sleep.

She thanked God for her and for everything He had provided for them in the last few weeks. Though much of that provision had come through the Kings, she knew that God had used them as channels of His blessing.

Even though she had no clue what the new year would hold, she did know that they would have a warm and safe place to live. She could handle anything else that might come their way as long as she had that for Rachel.

She ran her fingers lightly through Rachel's hair then brushed a kiss across her cheek before going around to her side of the bed and sliding under the blanket. Morning was going to come early. Of that, she had no doubt.

"Mama!" A small hand on her arm accompanied the word. "Mama!"

Carissa rolled over to look at Rachel in the mainly dark room, with only the nightlight casting any sort of illumination. "What's wrong?"

"Nothing! But I think Santa came." She gestured to the gifts on the table. "There are presents!"

Carissa glanced at the clock on the nightstand. 8:05 Well, Rachel had slept later than she had anticipated she would. Unfortunately, she'd forgotten to ask what time they should be downstairs. At least they could kill a little more time while Rachel opened the gifts on the nightstand.

"Can I open them, Mama?"

"Yes. You can." Carissa pushed herself up to sit against the headboard, then turned on the lamp.

"Yay!" Rachel reached over and picked up the top gift.

Settling down next to Carissa, Rachel began to remove the wrapping paper. Carissa knew that Rachel would be happy with what she'd gotten her. At least until she got downstairs and saw whatever Santa—AKA the Kings—had brought her.

For the next little while, Rachel oohed and awed over the coloring books, markers, books, clothes, and candy that Carissa had bought her.

"Can I have a piece of candy, Mama?"

Normally, she would have said absolutely not. But since one of the types of candies she'd gotten her were individually wrapped chocolates, she agreed that she could have just one.

After they'd cleaned up the wrapping paper and stacked the gifts on the small table next to the window, Carissa had Rachel wash up in the bathroom, then she fixed her hair. Once Rachel was ready, she had her sit at the table with a coloring book and markers while Carissa got ready.

They both stayed in their Christmas pajamas as per Heather's order, and just before nine o'clock, they made their way downstairs. Instead of going to the living room, even though Rachel looked longingly in that direction, Carissa guided her to the kitchen since she could smell coffee already.

"Merry Christmas!" Rachel called out to Essie as she skipped over to the woman.

"Merry Christmas, angel," Essie said, bending to give her a hug.

"Santa came!" Rachel said in a loud whisper.

"Yes. He did," Essie agreed.

Hunter walked in before Rachel could say anything more. Carissa stared at him and covered her mouth so that she didn't start to laugh. His Christmas pajamas were humorous, unlike the cute ones she and Rachel wore.

"No laughing allowed," Hunter muttered as he settled on a stool at the island.

"Did Heather get yours too?" Carissa asked.

"Do you think I would have chosen these for myself?" Hunter waved a hand up and down his body. "Shall we take bets on whether Hayden will have his pair on?"

"No betting on Christmas morning," Essie said. "But if we were, I'd say he won't."

Hunter nodded. "I'd agree with you."

"Well, then you'd both be wrong," Hayden said as he walked into the kitchen on his crutches.

Behind him came Heather and, a few minutes later, Eliza.

"Coffee," Essie announced as she began to pour from the carafe into the mugs that were already sitting on the counter. "And hot chocolate—well, warm chocolate—for the little angel."

Carissa thought maybe Rachel would protest, but she didn't. She just sat at the counter with Hunter and sipped from her mug. The others carried their mugs to the breakfast nook.

"Santa came, Mr. Hunter," Rachel said.

"Did he?"

She nodded. "He brought me coloring books, markers, books, and clothes. Oh, and candy! Mama let me have one small piece."

"Wow. That was nice of her." Hunter looked at Carissa and winked. "I don't think my mom would have let me have chocolate before breakfast. Even on Christmas."

"Did you check and see if he ate our cookies?"

Rachel shook her head. "Not yet."

"Well, let's finish our drinks, then we can go check."

"Are we going to have breakfast first?" Essie asked.

"I don't know if I can last that long," Hunter told her. "Maybe Rachel can check on the cookies, and we can open stockings, then eat breakfast."

Essie laughed as she gave a shake of her head. "I swear it's like you're experiencing a second childhood."

"I can't say you're wrong," Hunter said with a shrug. "And it's just as much fun this time around."

Once they'd finished with their drinks, Hunter took Rachel to the living room. Carissa followed them, wishing she had a way to take pictures because she really wanted to document this wonderful Christmas.

"Wow..." Rachel's steps slowed as she walked into the living room.

Carissa understood her reaction when she spotted the pile of presents that spilled out from under the tree. Even back when her parents had still been alive, they'd never had that many presents under the tree.

"Look at the cookies," Hunter said.

With clear reluctance, Rachel dragged her attention from the tree to where they'd left the plate of cookies.

"Why didn't he eat them all?" Rachel asked as she peered at the plate. "He just took a bite out of each one."

"I think he wanted to try them all, then he ate the one he liked the best."

"He ate mine!" She looked up at Hunter. "He ate mine, Mr. Hunter."

"I see that. I guess he liked yours the best."

"Mama, Santa liked my cookie best."

Hunter grinned at Carissa. "Yep. He really did like yours the best."

Carissa wasn't sure if Hunter had actually eaten it, but if he had, she was surprised he hadn't gone into sugar shock. Actually, she was pretty sure that Hunter *had* eaten the cookie. He seemed determined to make this experience as wonderful as possible for Rachel, even though she wouldn't know if he'd tossed her cookie into the garbage instead of eating it.

This man. Each day, he captured a bit more of her heart, and she didn't know what to do about it. If only he'd been a regular guy who worked a regular job. They might have had a chance at a relationship, but unfortunately, that wasn't who Hunter was. His job and lifestyle put him so far out of her reach.

They'd never made her feel less than equal because of her status in life, but she didn't really need them to do that when she already felt it all on her own.

The others joined them, and soon they were all settled with stockings in their laps. Carissa had thought they'd just do a stocking for Rachel, but there was one for each of them. Hayden gave Heather a skeptical look when she handed one to him.

"What's this?"

"A stocking. For some reason, Santa thought you deserved one, I guess."

"Haha," Hayden muttered.

Rachel clutched her stocking in her arms, her eyes wide. "Can I open it?"

"Yes, sweetheart," Heather said. "Go for it."

Carissa waited until everyone began to open their stockings before diving into hers. Inside it, she found an assortment of practical—if pricey—things. Small containers of expensive face care products along with lotions. A new brush. An electric toothbrush plus some toothpaste. There were also some chocolates and a pair of gloves that looked super warm.

"Thanks, sis..." Hunter coughed. "I mean, Santa really outdid himself."

Rachel had gotten some hand lotions that were made for little girls. She also had a new toothbrush and hairbrush. A lot of the same things Carissa had in her stocking, except with scents and designs for a little girl.

They hadn't even gotten to the presents yet, and Carissa was so grateful. Rachel also seemed thrilled with what she had already received, so Carissa couldn't imagine how she'd react to the gifts that were still under the tree.

How could she ever let this family know how grateful she was. *Thank you* just didn't seem enough. But what else did she have to show them her appreciation but her words? She had nothing to give them in return for all they'd done for her and Rachel.

Blinking rapidly against the sudden onset of moisture in her eyes, Carissa exhaled and looked down at the stocking in her lap. This Christmas had turned into everything she could have hoped for and so much more. Carissa knew that Rachel would never forget this time with the Kings, and neither would she.

CHAPTER 20

Hunter sensed that Carissa was feeling more than a little overwhelmed by everything. She had joined Rachel on the floor to help her with her presents after they'd eaten breakfast, obviously unaware that she would also be receiving quite a few. It wasn't until after Rachel had opened each of hers that Carissa had finally turned her attention to the stack beside her.

She paused for a moment before glancing up at Hunter, her brow furrowed. "These are for...*me*?"

"If they've got your name on them, I guess so. Santa must have decided that you were a good girl this year too."

"This is far too much," she said, without even opening one of the gifts. "You've already been so generous."

"Can't argue with Santa," Hayden told her gruffly. "And since he's not here to discuss it with, you might as well just open them."

Hunter almost laughed at the exasperated look Carissa gave his brother. She was clearly not as enamored with the idea of Santa as her daughter was.

"I'll help you open your presents, Mama," Rachel offered. "I can play with my presents later."

"It's okay, lovey," Carissa said, leaning over to hug her daughter. "I know you'd rather play with your presents."

Rachel nodded as she turned her attention back to the stack of books she'd opened earlier. It was clear she was happy her mom hadn't taken her up on her offer of help.

"Open your presents," Hunter said to Carissa.

She glanced at the small pile of stuff next to him. "You hardly got any presents."

"Guess that's a true reflection of his actions this year," Hayden commented. "Santa didn't bring him much at all."

"You're talking like you fared any better," Hunter tossed back at him.

"Be quiet, you two," Heather said. "Let Carissa open her presents in peace."

"Don't stop on my account," Carissa replied with a wave of her hand. "I admire how committed you are to the story."

Hunter moved to sit on the floor next to Carissa, lifting the stack of presents to the other side of him. He glanced at Heather and lifted a brow. As usual, she read his wordless question and joined him on the floor. After sorting through the presents, she handed him one, which he, in turn, handed to Carissa.

With a sigh, Carissa took it and set it in her lap to unwrap. Hunter had no idea what all Heather and his mom had bought her, so he watched curiously as she peeled away the Christmas paper.

"Can I give her one of my gifts next?" Rachel asked, apparently remembering that she'd also gotten some gifts for her mom.

Carissa looked up from the present she was unwrapping. "One of your gifts?"

Rachel smiled. "Yep! I went shopping and bought you stuff."

Carissa's shoulder slumped, but she didn't reply to Rachel's comment. Hunter knew that she wouldn't want to disappoint Rachel by saying something about her buying gifts.

Returning her attention to the box in her lap, Carissa peeled back the paper. Hunter was as in the dark as Carissa about what the wrapped presents contained.

"I don't know what you use for skincare," Heather said once the paper was removed. "But I've really liked that company. So I...uh....I mentioned to Santa that you might like it as well."

Hunter chuckled at Heather's near blunder. They really were going all out to keep the mystery of Santa alive for Rachel. His dad would have been happy about that.

"I usually just use soap and water," Carissa confessed. "So this is great."

Rachel scooted over to the stack of presents and pulled one out that was wrapped in bright green paper with Santa figures all over it. "I picked out the wrapping paper for you."

"Thank you, lovey," Carissa said as she took the present from her daughter.

Rachel was practically vibrating with excitement as she waited for Carissa to open it. "You can rip the paper, Mama."

Carissa gave a soft laugh. "You're so impatient."

"I want you to see what I got you."

Moving more quickly, Carissa removed the paper to reveal a box. She removed the lid, then lifted out what looked to be a light purple sweater.

"I got it cause it's my favorite color," Rachel explained. "And it is soooo soft."

Moving aside the box and paper, Carissa set the sweater on her lap and ran her hands over it. "It is very soft, and I love the color. Thank you."

Hunter knew that her thanks were extended beyond Rachel since she knew that her daughter wouldn't have had the money to purchase anything for her. There were two more presents for Carissa from Rachel. One was a silver necklace with two hearts on it that Rachel said represented her and Carissa. The last present was a purse, which Rachel reminded Carissa she needed since the strap on hers had broken months ago.

Carissa gathered Rachel close and gave her a tight hug. "All the presents are lovely. Thank you for picking them out for me."

Rachel beamed up at her mom as she pressed a kiss to her cheek. "I love you."

"Love you too."

"Now you can open the rest of your presents," Rachel instructed as she went back to her own stack.

Hunter watched as Carissa opened presents that contained several more pieces of clothing. Among them, there was new winterwear and a pair of black boots. The big-ticket items were left to the end, and he braced himself for her reaction, knowing that she was going to be even more overwhelmed when she opened them.

The problem was that they'd found it impossible to not want to shower the mother-daughter pair with everything they could possibly need. It would have been so easy to even buy her a new car to replace the one that wasn't working.

Instead, they'd had to restrain themselves—him especially—and just buy what was more practical. Though he still hoped that she'd let him arrange to have her car looked at and possibly repaired.

When she opened the new phone, her fingers brushed over the box before she looked over at him, her eyes awash in tears. "This is just too much."

Hunter didn't know what to say in response. For her, yes, it was a lot. Maybe too much. But for them? The phone and the laptop hadn't even put a dent in his bank account. He couldn't tell her that, though.

"You needed it," Heather said. "Rachel told us that you did."

"My phone works."

"But this is more than a phone." Hunter leaned over to take the box from her. "It's got a great camera, which is important when you have a kid like Rachel. You can record her life in pictures and videos."

He really wasn't above using Rachel yet again, and he'd use her once more when Carissa opened the laptop.

With quick movements, he opened the box to show her the rose gold-colored phone.

"It's so big," she said.

Compared to the little flip phone she'd been using, it was enormous. Hunter wondered how to tell her that he'd set up a new plan to go along with the phone, but he decided that he could reveal that later.

"Here." Heather held out her hand to him, and Hunter laid the phone in it. "Let me transfer all the pictures that we've taken so far of Rachel. It's really easy to do."

While Heather did that, Carissa turned her attention to the last present, looking at it like it was a snake poised to bite her. She glanced up at Hunter as she took the heavy gift from him.

"I don't even want to think about what this is," Carissa murmured.

"Well, this one is definitely from Santa since it was on Rachel's list."

"The Santa excuse doesn't work as well on me as it does on her," Carissa said with a small smile. "But nice try."

Hunter leaned back against the couch and crossed his arms. "I'm sticking with the Santa story."

"Such a convenient excuse," Carissa told him.

"It's worked wonderfully this year, I have to say." He gave her a smile. "Now open your present."

With a shake of her head, she began to unwrap the paper from around the large flat box. When she pulled the paper away enough to reveal what it was, she gave a big sigh.

"Hunter," she reproved. "Dare I say that it's too much?"

"You can dare, but it won't matter. Santa made that decision. Ask Rachel if you don't believe me. It was on her list."

"He's right, Mama," Rachel said. "I asked Santa for a new laptop for you since your old one doesn't work very well. I'm glad he brought that since he didn't bring the other thing I asked for you."

Hunter almost laughed when Carissa said, "What was the other thing?"

"I asked him to bring you a husband."

Carissa's jaw dropped, and Hunter could see a flush of pink on her cheek. "A...husband?"

"Yep," Rachel said with a nod. "You need a husband. Someone to help you and make you happy."

"You make me happy, lovey. I don't need a husband."

"But Ally at school says her dad does stuff for her mom that makes her happy. I want that for you."

"Well, I appreciate the idea," Carissa said. "But I think a husband was probably not something that Santa could get me."

Rachel leaned against her, a frown on her face. "How else will you get one?"

"I'm not sure, but he's not going to come from Santa, I'm pretty sure."

Hunter smiled at the pair, wishing he could reveal his romantic interest in Carissa, but he knew that the timing wasn't great. He was sure that Rachel liked him and wouldn't object if he and her mom dated. However, he didn't want her to pressure Carissa into anything.

This situation had to be handled with care, and Hunter didn't want to risk blowing things before he even got a chance to tell her how he felt.

~*~

Carissa wasn't sure how to deal with...well, everything. The stockings. The gifts for Rachel. The gifts for her. The place to stay. She couldn't even begin to name everything the Kings had done for her and Rachel.

She didn't know what to say in order to convey to them how thankful she was. Just a few weeks ago, she had been so certain that with the pending move, Christmas that year was going to be the worst one yet. Instead, it was going to be one of their best.

Though the gifts played a part in that, it wasn't the main part as far as Carissa was concerned. For her, it had been the friendship offered to them and the opportunity to worship together the night before. And the day wasn't even over yet.

In the future, she would certainly remember this as the Christmas she received amazing presents. But more than that, she'd remember it as the Christmas when a special family had offered them friendship. And in the midst of a shared sorrow, they'd been able to bring joy to each other.

She thought that maybe this time with the Kings would be a turning point for all of them. They'd been struggling with their grief, just as she had. It seemed that they had been able to fulfill needs for each other.

Carissa glanced over to where Hunter sat with her phone in his hand. She still couldn't believe that they'd bought her a phone...and a laptop...and so much more.

"You'll have a new number with this phone," Hunter said as he tapped something on the screen. "I've already input all our numbers into your contact list, so you can call or text us if you need something."

"I think you've made sure that we're not going to need anything," Carissa told him.

Hunter smiled at her. "Okay. Then maybe you could call us just to talk. You don't need a reason to call any of us."

"You might regret removing the qualifier that I need something in order to call you. And you'd better be prepared for calls from Rachel if you give an open invitation to do so."

"I know you're probably joking, but just so you know, if I don't hear from you or Rachel regularly, I'll be blowing up your phone."

Carissa wasn't sure how to react to his statement. At times, some of the things he said seemed flirtatious, but she wasn't one hundred percent sure that was how he meant it. And if it was, she had no idea what to do with that.

Early on, her focus had been on her baby and her studies for nursing school, and then it had been on trying to survive after her parents' death and providing for her daughter. The only flirting she'd dealt with of late had been from the older gentlemen who frequented the restaurant.

Hunter was definitely not an elderly gentleman, which made it hard to not want to take his flirting seriously. Still, on the off chance he *was* serious, Carissa didn't know what to think.

Her heart said to toss caution to the wind and ignore the potential issues. It was very tempting, but she had Rachel to think about. She would be devastated if Carissa allowed things to develop with Hunter, but then they didn't work out. It would be hard to stay in the Kings' lives in that situation. Their friendships were too important to risk.

But what if things did *work out with Hunter? What if I give him a chance, and he turns out to be the wonderful man that I think he is?*

Those questions warred with her caution, and Carissa was glad that Hunter wasn't asking her to go out with him right then because she wouldn't know what to say.

"Let's set up your face," Hunter said as he moved a bit closer to her.

"Set up my face?"

"Yep. That way, your phone stays locked until it recognizes your face."

"Seriously?"

"Seriously," he said with a grin.

"I guess I haven't been paying too much attention to the latest versions of these phones. I focused on whatever was cheapest and allowed me to be contacted by the school or my work."

"You'll have to give them your new number," Hunter said. "Also, if you'd like, I'd be okay with you adding me as an emergency contact for Rachel, in case there's ever a time they are unable to get hold of you."

Carissa lowered the phone and stared at him. "You'd like to be an emergency contact for her?"

"I would, and I think she'd be okay if I had to pick her up instead of you, right? If you needed me to?"

"She'd definitely be okay with that."

"Anyway, I wanted to make the offer. You don't have to tell me now. Just give me a head's up if you decide to do it."

"It would be a wise thing to do, I think. It's always been in the back of my mind that I have no one to step in and care for Rachel if something should happen to me. It used to be my parents who were there as my backup, but I haven't found anyone that I trust since they were killed."

"I hope I've proven that I'm willing to step in and take responsibility for Rachel."

Carissa nodded. "You really have. I bet you didn't expect that you'd end up there when you knocked on our apartment door that day with Mr. Edgemire."

"That's very true," Hunter said with a thoughtful expression on his face. Carissa had a hard time believing that she'd once thought of him as stern. "But I don't regret it one little bit. Which is why I'd be honored if you'd accept me as an emergency contact for Rachel and for you too."

Carissa knew that she'd be stupid to not take him up on his offer. Rachel deserved to know that if something happened to Carissa, she would be taken care of by people she trusted. She'd clearly felt comfortable with them when Carissa had ended up in the hospital.

"I'll let the school know."

Hunter smiled at her, making Carissa feel like he really did consider it an honor to play that role for her and Rachel. Plus, his offer made it seem like she and Rachel weren't just a Christmas charity project for the family.

They'd just finished with the phone when Essie called them to the dining room for their Christmas dinner. Rachel skipped ahead of them, then plunked herself in the chair that Essie directed her to. Carissa was on one side, and Heather was on Rachel's other.

When Essie told Hunter to sit on Carissa's other side, she wondered if perhaps a matchmaker was at work. Eliza smiled at her as she sat down at the head of the table, and Carissa thought maybe there might be two matchmakers.

Once they were all seated at the beautifully decorated table laden with food, Eliza beamed around at each of them. "This has been a wonderful Christmas, and I'm so thankful to have a couple new faces at the table who have become wonderful friends. I look forward to spending more time with you both in the future. Thank you for bringing such joy to our lives and our home this year."

As Eliza said a prayer of thanks, Carissa blinked back tears as love flooded her heart for each of these people. Love for the ones who had become friends. And love for the one who was becoming so much more.

CHAPTER 21

Hunter sank onto the loveseat in front of the fireplace, where the fire had been stoked by the addition of another log. A quiet had settled over the house as people had retreated to their rooms after a full day of activities.

It had been a good day, one that Hunter knew he'd remember for many years to come. For the first time in four years, they'd actually celebrated Christmas. In recent years, they'd gone through the motions. Trees had been decorated. Presents had been purchased and wrapped. A turkey dinner had been prepared and eaten. But it had all felt hollow, overlaid with sadness because a vital part of their family was missing.

They'd continued to celebrate the true meaning of the season—Christ's birth—but it had been the other parts of Christmas that had dimmed in joy. Hunter was sure that each year the others had been as eager for the holiday to be over as he'd been.

This year, though, he was sad that it was over. He'd thoroughly enjoyed spending the holiday with his family and with Carissa and Rachel. It felt like joy had been infused back into their family, and he wasn't sure what would happen now that the holiday was over. It wouldn't be long until the pair were settled into their new apartment, and Hunter likely wouldn't see them on a daily basis like he had been recently.

Motion near the entrance of the room drew his attention from the flickering fire. He smiled when he saw Carissa enter the room and head over to where he sat.

"Hey, there," he said. "I thought you were upstairs for the night."

She dropped down on the loveseat beside him. "I was, but I came down to get something to drink. Rachel dropped right off, and since she's more familiar with the house now, I figured I was safe to leave the room for a few minutes."

"Were you looking for someone?"

"You mean because I ended up here after the kitchen?" Hunter nodded. "Well, I smelled the smoke and thought I'd see if the fire was still burning."

"I added another log when I came in here. If you'd like to be alone with the fire, I can leave."

"No," Carissa said quickly, holding out her hand. "No. I'm glad for the company. Your company."

"Well, I'm glad because I'm happy to have your company too," Hunter said, angling himself so he faced her more fully. "Did you have a good day?"

Carissa lifted her brows. "Are you really asking me that?"

"So it was either that good or that bad," Hunter said.

"Definitely that good," Carissa assured him. "The only thing that could possibly have made it any better would have been if your dad and my parents had been here with us."

Hunter nodded. "The sad thing is, I'm not sure our paths would have crossed if they were still alive."

Carissa frowned at his words. "I suppose that's true. Now that we've gotten to know you, I would hate to have to give up your friendship."

"I guess we just need to be grateful for the path God has led us on, even though it was sorrow and loss that started us on the journey to meeting each other."

It seemed his words had a positive effect on Carissa because the frown eased from her expression, and a smile took its place. "God knew that we needed each other. Though obviously, we needed you more than you needed us."

"I'm not so sure about that," Hunter said. "You and Rachel have brought us priceless gifts. The gifts of joy and love."

"I know you say that," Carissa began, her gaze going past him to the fire. "But I still feel like you've given us so much. On top of all the gifts, you helped us find a place to live."

Hunter nodded. "I'm glad that we've been able to help you on a practical level. I know that a new apartment was particularly important to you. But seeing the smile on my mom's face over this past week has been incredible. I think that's the most I've seen her smile—genuinely, anyway—since my dad passed away. That's the gift that you gave my siblings and me."

Carissa's gaze met his then, emotion filling her expression. "I'm so glad. It feels like you've given us so much, and we hadn't given you anything in return."

"Don't ever think that," Hunter told her. "And don't think that now that Christmas is over that you're not going to see us anymore. You're too important for us to just let you go. Expect invites to dinner at least once a week, followed by plenty of phone calls and text messages."

Hunter hesitated before continuing on. "And my mom and Heather would be happy to babysit Rachel if you'd like to go out sometime."

"Go out? Like on a date?" Carissa asked with a laugh. "I don't have anyone asking me out on a date these days."

"And if you did?"

Carissa's brow furrowed. "Well, I guess my response would depend on who was doing the asking."

"Me," Hunter said. "What would your answer be if I asked you out?"

Her eyes widened. "Is that a...a joke?"

"Why would it be a joke?"

"You could ask anyone out. Why would you ask someone like me?"

"First of all, why *wouldn't* I ask someone like you? You're amazing."

"It's just that I don't have anything to offer."

"I think we've just discussed that you do, in fact, have plenty to offer. You're also raising an amazing daughter who, just by sharing her joy, has plenty to offer. I know that it's the disparity in our financial statuses that is probably causing you concern. I don't mean to be dismissive of that because I know that it's easy for me to say that it doesn't matter."

Carissa nodded. "I know that I shouldn't judge you by your financial situation, just like I wouldn't want to be judged by mine."

"Exactly," Hunter agreed. "I would hope that I have more to offer someone than just my money."

Carissa's look turned contemplative, but she didn't say anything.

"Now, if you think I'm a total schmuck that you can't wait to see the back of, that's a completely different story. In that case, feel free to tell me to back off."

She shook her head vigorously. "No. I don't feel that way about you at all. I really...really like you, and I've enjoyed the time I've spent with you."

Hunter was relieved to hear that. "Enough to spend some more time together? Maybe just the two of us this time?"

Her smile warmed Hunter's heart and gave him hope. "I'd like that."

"You'd want to go on a date with me?" He needed to be sure they were on the same page and that she wasn't agreeing to just hang out as friends.

"I'd love to," she said with an expression that looked like affection on her face.

Hunter hoped he wasn't just reading into things because of what he wanted. "Maybe we can go out tomorrow night. Or is that too soon?"

"It's not too soon, but I can't guarantee that Rachel won't want to come with us. I think you're one of her favorite people."

"Mom and Heather would come up with something fun for her to do with them."

"I'm sure that would make her happy."

"Any preferences on where we should go?" Hunter asked.

"The last time I dated anyone, I was barely out of high school. Anything you plan will be fine with me. Just no rock concerts."

Hunter laughed. "Okay. No rock concerts."

Carissa was extremely grateful that Heather had given her some clothes for Christmas and that she'd judged the sizes correctly. She wasn't sure that her own clothes would have been good enough for wherever Hunter was taking her, even though he had said to dress casually. Had Heather bought her the clothes because she knew that Hunter wanted to date her?

Carissa still wasn't sure that dating Hunter was the best idea. But when she'd realized that he actually wanted to go out on a date with her, her heart had overridden her mind.

He'd been right that it was his money that gave her pause. If he'd just been an average guy with an average job, she probably wouldn't have thought twice about accepting his invitation.

What if he'd been reluctant to date her because she didn't have money? How was that any better than her feeling that way because he *did* have money?

Carissa knew other qualities were more important than Hunter's wealth, but she still wanted to lay down some guidelines. Like no dates that involved taking private jets or anything like that.

Hopefully, wherever they were going that night would be a place that would ease her into dating a wealthy man. If Hunter couldn't see that it would be nerve-wracking for her to be thrown right into the upper echelon of society, then them dating would never work.

"Are you sure that you don't want to come with Heather and me to the movie?"

Carissa smiled at Rachel as she picked up her purse. "Maybe another time."

Rachel talked animatedly about the movie they were going to. It had been fortunate that a new family movie released over Christmas that Rachel was eager to see.

Downstairs, Heather was ready to go since the two were going to have an early dinner before the movie. Carissa helped Rachel into her winter wear, tugging the knit cap over her hair.

"You be good for Heather, okay?" she said.

"I'll be very good."

"Have fun." Carissa gave her a kiss. "I'll see you later."

She watched the two walk out to where George waited for them. Heather wasn't a big fan of driving, Carissa had discovered. Especially when the weather wasn't the greatest.

Hunter appeared a moment later, a smile on his face. He was dressed in jeans and a long-sleeve T-shirt, making her feel better about her own jeans and sweater. She still had to wonder if casual applied when the clothes cost a fortune.

"Ready to go?" Hunter asked.

"Yep." She was equal parts excited and worried about where they might be going. But she figured that where they ended up for their date would be a good indication of how much Hunter considered her when making his plans.

They pulled on their jackets, then headed out to where Hunter's SUV was warming up. Hunter opened the passenger door, then closed it again once Carissa was in her seat.

"So, are you going to tell me where we're going?" Carissa asked as Hunter drove the SUV down the driveway and out onto the street.

"Not yet," he told her. "But I promise you're going to like it."

"Have you been there yourself?"

"Not yet. This was recommended to me by someone at the office, and they said it was great. If you enjoy it, maybe we can bring Rachel some time."

They chatted about what Rachel was doing with Heather, and it felt so normal to be talking with Hunter like that. Carissa felt more comfortable with him than she might have thought she would if someone had presented this scenario to her before she'd gotten to know the King family.

"We're going to the Mall of America?" Carissa asked as Hunter turned into the parking lot of the huge building.

"Yes, we are."

Carissa could only imagine one thing there that would be interesting to Rachel, and she wasn't sure how she felt about it. An amusement park wasn't something she'd ever really enjoyed, though she was sure Rachel would love it.

Once he'd parked, they headed toward the entrance to the mall. Hunter offered her his arm as they walked, which Carissa gladly took since there were icy patches on the sidewalk that led to the doors.

They were greeted by warmth and people busy shopping for after-Christmas sales. Hunter skillfully guided them through the mall in the direction of the amusement park, and Carissa braced herself for the noise that was to come.

As they walked through the part of the mall devoted to the amusement park, Hunter seemed to have a particular destination in mind because they didn't stop to buy tickets at any of the rides they passed. When it seemed their destination was in sight, Carissa was still in the dark about what it was.

"I hope you like this," Hunter said as they fell into line behind several other people.

"What exactly is it?" Carissa asked, taking in the name next to the entrance.

"From what I've read and from what the guy at work said, it's an amazing experience that mimics flying over the country. It's enhanced by the use of mist and scents."

"I've never flown before, so this should be interesting."

Hunter laughed. "I have flown before, but I have a feeling this isn't going to be anything like that. I'm looking forward to it."

Carissa thought that this was a ride she could enjoy. She eagerly listened to all the instructions and then followed Hunter to where they sat down beside each other, facing a large screen.

After they were all settled and secure, Hunter leaned close and said, "I hope that this meets your approval for our date."

"So far, so good," she assured him, smiling to let him know that she was enjoying their time together.

In all honesty, she was just happy to be anywhere with him. Since the moment he'd expressed an interest in dating her, she'd let down the wall she'd erected around her heart, believing that the feelings she had for Hunter would never be returned.

232 · KIMBERLY RAE JORDAN

Was it too soon to name her feelings as love? She'd seen different sides of him since the first time they'd met, and each and every one of them was admirable. He took the responsibility of his family care seriously, doing what he could to be a rock for his mom. And he was always expressing his concern for Hayden—who had returned to their apartment earlier that afternoon.

Carissa didn't want her and Rachel to become just one more responsibility for him, though their acquaintance had started out that way. But so far, she didn't feel like that was the case, especially since everything had been settled with regards to their housing need. They'd have a new home to go to soon, and Hunter wouldn't be responsible for their actual care any longer. Then they could just have a friendship...and more.

The ride began, and Carissa could say that as far as rides went, it was something beyond all her expectations. Her smile only grew through the experience, and when it was over, she felt a keen sense of disappointment that it hadn't lasted much, much longer.

She glanced up at Hunter as they exited the ride and noticed how the smile on his face made him look younger than usual.

"That was amazing."

He looked at her, his smile growing. "It was, wasn't it? Want to go again?"

"Can we?"

His eyes sparkled as he nodded. He reached out and took her hand, and together, they went back to get in line for the ride again.

"You'll have to thank the guy at work," Carissa said. "His recommendation was terrific."

"I'm going to get him a gift card or something. I just wish the ride was longer."

"I felt the same way." Carissa leaned her head against his arm. "I loved it so much, and I think Rachel would love it too. We need to bring her and Heather next time. Do you think Hayden would come with us?"

Hunter shrugged. "Maybe. I'll have to ask him."

Carissa thought that it would be a great family outing. "We could bring your mom, Essie, and George as well."

Hunter let go of her hand to slip his arm around her shoulders, pulling her close against him. "I'm so glad that you want to spend time with my family and with me."

"Your family means a lot to me, and I've enjoyed all the time we've spent together."

"I'm glad because I think we're going to be together a lot."

Carissa was glad to hear that. Joy filled her as she imagined them together in the future. Her heart was filled with more love than she'd ever imagined possible. And finally, the love she held for her parents could exist without the anger and grief that had weighed her down for the past four years. With their new apartment being a safe place for her and Rachel, she could focus on enjoying life instead of just existing.

And though the circumstances they'd met under hadn't been the greatest, she was glad for the journey that God had guided them on because it had brought her to this amazing man and his wonderful   family.

CHAPTER 22

On New Year's Eve, Carissa spent some time throughout the day reflecting back on the year. It was the first time since her parents' death that she was ending the year in a better place than she'd started it.

Just a few short weeks ago, she'd anticipated that this was going to be the worst end of a year since that awful year she'd lost her parents. Instead, she had been given a chance, an opportunity to move in an upward direction instead of continuing on the downward slide she'd been on for what felt like forever.

She wouldn't take it for granted. Though she'd questioned God a lot over the years, especially regarding the circumstances around her parents' death, she was discovering that He hadn't abandoned her, even though she'd felt like He had.

Carissa had felt like she had no one to turn to. No one to help her when life was threatening to pull her under. But God had still been there for her. Working in ways she couldn't have imagined. Even now, looking back over the past couple of weeks, she was still in awe of how everything had unfolded.

"Are you almost ready, Mama?" Rachel asked from where she stood in the doorway of the bathroom.

Carissa dropped the lipstick she'd been using into the cosmetic bag—all of it courtesy of Heather—and turned to face her daughter. Rachel wore a dark blue velvet and satin dress, and her hair was up in a ponytail with a bow and fashioned into ringlets. Again, with Heather's help.

Her own outfit was something Eliza had given her. The woman had shown up at her room earlier in the week with an armful of dresses, insisting that they were all for Carissa. Thankfully, Eliza's personal style tended toward the timeless, so even though she'd had the dresses for many years, they didn't look like they were out of fashion.

Heather had offered her some dresses, but they'd all agreed that Eliza's were the better choice since Heather had a few inches on Carissa. Heather had also pointed out that Carissa's build overall was closer to Eliza's, with both of them having a more slender and petite body type.

In the end, Eliza had been more than happy to pass on quite a few things, while Heather teased her about finally cleaning out her closet. Eliza had brushed aside her daughter's comments, telling her that all she'd needed was a good reason to tackle it.

Carissa had been the lucky recipient of more clothes than she could possibly wear. But thankfully, in amongst those clothes had been several that were appropriate for that evening's festivities.

The dress she had chosen was a black satin number with a lace overlay on the skirt. It had a scoop neck and long sleeves. It was a very simple style, but when she'd tried it on, it had made her feel amazing. She didn't care that it was second-hand. In fact, it made her feel better about accepting the clothing.

Eliza had even had a brand new pair of black heels that she'd purchased at one point but never worn. She'd looked a little embarrassed when she'd admitted that.

Carissa didn't begrudge the Kings their wealth. From everything she'd heard, the elder King had worked very hard to build a fortune so that he could offer his family a life very different from the one he'd had growing up. But she'd learned it was more than that. He wanted to be able to help others—through offering them jobs, places to live, education, and more.

It didn't escape her attention that before he'd died, Hunter's father had unknowingly laid the groundwork for where she was that day. More than once, she'd thanked God for the person who had raised the man she loved, instilling in him a sense of family and responsibility. Things she really admired about Hunter.

That night, Carissa was going to have that amazing man at her side as they rang in the New Year, and she couldn't wait.

"Let's go, lovey," Carissa said as she stepped out of the bathroom.

"Finally!"

Rachel skipped ahead of her toward the door of their bedroom. Carissa hadn't been sure about including Rachel in the evening since it was going to run past midnight, but Heather had assured her that it would be fine. They'd even reserved a suite in the hotel where the party was being held, and Heather had said she'd take Rachel up there if she got tired.

Downstairs, she found Heather and Hunter waiting in the living room.

"Look at you!" Heather exclaimed. "You both look lovely."

"I agree," Hunter said. "You look very beautiful."

Rachel spun in a circle. "I love my dress!"

Carissa stepped close to Hunter, who looked very handsome in his dark gray suit with a black and silver patterned tie.

"Well don't you two look amazing together," Heather said. "I'm jealous."

"What are you jealous about?" Carissa asked. "You're stunning."

Heather waved a hand dismissively. "I'm jealous that you two found each other. I'd love to have a handsome man on my arm for the evening."

"There are plenty of good-looking guys who would have accompanied you tonight," Hunter said. "I've had many of them ask me how to get your attention."

Heather grimaced. "Okay. I don't want a handsome date. I want a *nice* one. Not a guy whose gaze is on my wallet instead of my face. Who's only being nice to me because they want my money. I don't need a guy like that, even if he's the most handsome man on earth."

"Then you'll need to date a guy with more money than you."

Heather shook her head. "That's rather limiting. I'd rather just find a guy who doesn't care about my money. Who would say that even if I lost every single penny of my wealth, he'd still want to be with me."

"All you can do is keep living and pray that God brings that guy into your life," Hunter told her. "You never know when you might stumble across him."

"I doubt it will be tonight," Heather said. "Instead, I'll make sure Rachel has a good time."

"Thank you for doing that," Carissa said. "I know she's going to have a wonderful evening."

The sound of voices preceded the appearance of Eliza, Essie, and George, who were all dressed to the nines. After some moments of mutual admiration, they all pulled on their warm outer clothes and headed out to the limo that had been hired for the evening.

"That's a *big* car, Mama," Rachel said when she spotted it.

Carissa agreed with her observation as they headed toward the limo. It was kind of nice that neither George nor Hunter had to drive that night. The only one missing from the family was Hayden. However, the man had made it clear earlier that day that there was no way on earth that he would attend the New Year's Eve party.

Heather went into the limo first, then helped her mom and Essie to climb inside. Carissa and Rachel went next, followed by George and Hunter. As soon as they were all seated, the limo began to move, smoothly driving around the circular driveway and out onto the street.

Carissa found her nervousness increasing as the limo drove them to their destination. This was a party put on by the Kings, so there was likely to be a focus on the family that night. And since they were with them, that focus might end up on her and Rachel too.

Would people be able to tell that she didn't move in the same financial sphere as the Kings? Would they think that Hunter could do so much better than a single mom who waited tables?

"Everything is going to be fine." Hunter's voice wrapped around her as he leaned close.

She looked over at him. "How do you know I'm worried?"

"I know you," Hunter said. "We've spent enough time together over the past several weeks for me to know that you're likely worried about the evening."

She nodded. "This is so very different from anything that I've ever been to."

"You do realize that this isn't a party put on for fellow rich folks, right? The people attending are employees of our company, and we put this on for them. Just like the children's party is for the kids of our employees, this is a party for the adults."

"I'll try to keep that in mind."

"Just try to enjoy yourself. I'll be right there with you," Hunter said. "But if you need a break, feel free to escape to the suite we've reserved."

Carissa nodded, wanting only to make Hunter happy and to celebrate the new year with the Kings. At least it seemed that Rachel wasn't nervous at all about attending, though it didn't sound like there was going to be any other kids there.

Once they arrived at the hotel, they exited the limo and headed inside. Heather took charge of Rachel, holding her hand as they headed to the ballroom. Carissa happily slid her hand into Hunter's when he offered it to her, letting go only when they had to take off their coats at the coat-check that had been set up for the evening.

After that was done, she took his hand again, then stared around in awe. The room's overhead lights were set on a low level, and there looked to be thousands of fairy lights hanging from the ceiling. Tables ringed the room, each with a lovely centerpiece of flowers and candles. The theme seemed to be blue and silver with black accents. It was truly lovely.

For the next hour, she and Hunter circled the room, speaking to people, many of whom Hunter greeted by name. Either he had an amazing memory, or he interacted regularly with these people at work.

Given what she knew of his position in the company, it would be understandable if he didn't interact with people in every department. However, it was clear he did because the people responded to his greetings with familiar friendliness. They didn't seem to be in awe of him as a member of the family who founded the company.

"They all love you," Carissa murmured as they moved away from the group of people they'd just been talking with.

Hunter squeezed her hand and grinned. "What's not to love?"

That made her laugh. "Well, there were a couple ladies who seemed not to love me standing next to you. I feel like they think you should have picked from the local pool rather than looking in a different one."

"That wasn't going to happen," Hunter said. "First of all, because no one had ever caught my eye. Secondly, it's never good to date an employee."

"But it's okay to date a landlord?"

"Definitely."

She smiled at him, then leaned her head against his shoulder. "This really is an amazing event. Thank you for inviting me."

"I had to," Hunter said. "Because there's no one else I'd rather be with to ring in the New Year."

Her heart swelled with all the love she felt for the man, and she understood exactly how he felt. A growing part of her hoped that this new year was the first of many they would celebrate together.

~*~

Hunter had attended the New Year's Eve company party for most of his adult life, but he'd never enjoyed any of them as much as he did the one that night. With Carissa at his side, he happily made his rounds of the room, stopping to chat with the employees and their dates. He was thrilled to be able to introduce Carissa to everyone they spoke to.

Some might suspect that she was just his date for the evening, but nothing could be further from the truth. He was very, very serious about Carissa, and he hoped she was also serious about him.

They had joined the rest of the family at a table for the dinner. It was a tasty meal, but that was no surprise because his mom only used caterers who met her exacting standards for food quality.

The large space in the center of the room was filled with people dancing, but Hunter didn't ask Carissa to join him there. He was not a dancer by any stretch of the imagination, and Carissa didn't seem disappointed that they would not be joining the crowd.

Heather did take Rachel out on the dancefloor, however, and the pair seemed to be having plenty of fun, even though it was well past the little girl's bedtime. He had thought Heather would have to take her up to the suite, which was the main reason they'd reserved it. But as the time clicked closer to midnight, Rachel showed no sign of tiring.

Soon, the DJ they'd hired for the evening announced that it was twenty minutes until midnight and that if people wanted to get a drink to toast the New Year in, now was the time to do it.

Servers began circulating through the room with trays of drinks. They offered champagne along with sparkling white grape juice for people who preferred not to drink alcohol. Knowing that his mom preferred the grape juice, and it was what Rachel would have to drink, Hunter had a server bring that for each of them at the table.

The lights in the room had been lowered even further after the meal, though the myriad fairy lights cast plenty of illumination so people could move safely around the room. Hunter and Carissa were alone at the table, but they wouldn't be for long.

"Have you had a good evening?" he asked, angling himself to face her more fully.

She smiled at him. "It's been wonderful. Better than I had expected, to be honest. I was a bit nervous about this."

"I know. I could tell." He took her hand and held it in both of his. "But I'm so glad you're here with me tonight. It makes the evening even more special."

"It's been the best New Year's Eve I've ever had. I'm really looking forward to the year ahead."

"So am I. Normally, I don't look toward a new year with any great excitement or expectation. But this year, I can't wait to see what the next twelve months hold for me. For us."

"I'm looking forward to that too."

Hunter paused before lifting her hand to press a kiss to the back of it. "We haven't known each other very long. But because of the time we've spent together, I feel like I've gotten to know you quite well."

"You certainly got a crash course on the life of Carissa and Rachel when you knocked on our door."

"That's not something I will ever regret. In fact, I'm glad that I was so anxious to get out of the office that day that I went to your building."

When Carissa's smile deepened, Hunter's heart skipped a beat. Whether she knew it or not, this woman held his heart, and he could no longer imagine a future without her and Rachel in it. Nor did he want to.

He wasn't worried about having fallen in love with her over a matter of weeks. It had been the same with his parents. If Hunter could believe his dad, it had been love at first sight for him. However, he knew that other people might not have the same experience and might not feel comfortable with hearing about love so soon. If that was the case for Carissa, he'd hold off on telling her about how he felt.

But first, he had to know.

"Will I scare you off if I tell you how I feel about you?" Hunter wanted so much to share what was in his heart, but not if she wasn't ready to hear it.

Her eyes widened, and her lips parted as she stared at him for a long moment. A very long moment. "How you feel?"

"Yes. I want to share that with you, but only if you're ready to hear it."

Her expression relaxed as she smiled at him. "Oh Hunter, unless you're going to tell me you don't want me around anymore, I think I'm more than ready to hear what you have to say."

"I'll never tell you that. Never." He ran his fingertips down her cheek, enjoying how her eyes sparkled with the reflection of the fairy lights. "You are too important to me for that. I love you, Carissa, and I want to start the new year knowing that we're both serious about being together."

Carissa leaned closer to him. "I love you too, Hunter. Even though you rescued us, and I'll always be grateful for that, I've come to realize that you are a truly wonderful man. I love your giving heart. I love seeing how you care for your family. I love how you want to carry on your dad's legacy. You're just so incredible, and I'm so blessed that you love me."

"I'm the blessed one," Hunter argued. "From the moment we first met, I could see that you would do anything for your daughter. Even though you've experienced tragedy and loss, you're still so loving." He paused. "I know you were probably as close to rock bottom as you'd ever been the day we met, and I'm sorry for the role I played in that."

"No." Carissa shook her head. "No. You're not allowed to feel guilty about that. You had the best of intentions with what you were doing, and you gave us plenty of time to move out. It wasn't your fault that I couldn't find a place. I don't want there to be any guilt in our relationship."

It hurt his heart to think about what Carissa and Rachel had endured before he'd knocked on their door that day. But Carissa was right. He needed to let the guilt go and embrace the joy and love she and Rachel had brought into his life.

When the DJ announced fewer than five minutes until midnight, the other family members returned to the table. They all grabbed a glass, then got to their feet. Soon, the DJ began to lead them in the countdown.

Rachel danced around with excitement, yelling out the seconds with everyone else. As they reached zero, *Auld Lang Syne* began to play as people toasted and kissed.

244 · KIMBERLY RAE JORDAN

"May I kiss you?" Hunter asked as he leaned close to Carissa after setting their glasses on the nearby table.

When she smiled and lifted her face, Hunter took a moment to appreciate what this meant for them. He bent to press his lips to hers, then wrapped his arms around her.

Joy suffused him, and Hunter said a prayer of thanks to God for freeing him and his family from the grip of sorrow and grief. They would have gotten there eventually, or at least he hoped they would have, but God had used a single mom and her daughter to hasten that day.

Hunter prayed that God's joy and love would continue to infuse their lives for years to come, in seasons of happiness and in seasons of sorrow. Though selfishly, he did hope that there would be more happiness than sorrow with Carissa and Rachel by his side.

He hadn't known the joy and love that awaited him behind the door of a rundown apartment in a derelict building. God had truly guided their paths, through sorrow and grief, to bring them into each other's lives and hearts. Though his dad wasn't there to rejoice with them, Hunter knew that through all of them—Carissa and Rachel included—his legacy would live on.

~*~ The End ~*~

Be sure to check out Book 2 of this series:

CHILD OF LOVE

ABOUT THE AUTHOR

Kimberly Rae Jordan is a USA Today bestselling author of Christian romances. Many years ago, her love of reading Christian romance morphed into a desire to write stories of love, faith, and family, and thus began a journey that would lead her to places Kimberly never imagined she'd go.

In addition to being a writer, she is also a wife and mother, which means Kimberly spends her days straddling the line between real life in a house on the prairies of Canada and the imaginary world her characters live in. Though caring for her husband and four kids and working on her stories takes up a large portion of her day, Kimberly also enjoys reading and looking at craft ideas that she will likely never attempt to make.

As she continues to pen heartwarming stories of love, faith, and family, Kimberly hopes that readers of all ages will enjoy the journeys her characters take in each book. She has no plan to stop writing the stories God places on her heart and looks forward to where her journey will take her in the years to come.